DON'T WANT NO MAN

DON'T NEED NO MAN

AIN'T GOT NO MAN

Also featuring the stories:
THE LEFT HAND... THIRD FINGER
SAVING THE LAST DANCER

Author: A.e. Santi

This book is a compilation of short stories from the brilliant mind of A.e. Santi. It includes these three compelling and captivating stories:

DON'T WANT NO MAN
DON'T NEED NO MAN
AIN'T GOT NO MAN
COPYRIGHT 2015
SAVING THE LAST DANCER
COPYRIGHT 2015
THE LEFT HAND... THIRD FINGER
COPYRIGHT 2015

Here are other books that will be available soon:

A BLACK WOMAN'S TRUST: BOUGHT & BETRAYED

ONE MAN SEPARATED

FROM P.I. TO P.I.

TOUCHED

Watch out for these upcoming books from the "DYNASTY" series:
IN MY FATHER'S STEPS
STEPPING INTO A DYNASTY
CLASH OF A DYNASTY
FALL OF A DYNASTY
DYNASTY RESURRECTED

Don't want no man… Don't need no
man…Ain't got no man

Chapter One

It was mid-summer and Precious, what her
mother had thought enough of her at birth,
seemed to always be in the middle of doing
something for, to , or with any of the four
kids that she had naturally given birth to--
starting with her first one eight years ago.
Seemed they'd kept coming every two years
after that.

"Y'all better stop all that damn noise right
now 'fo I come in there and beat *all* y'all
asses!" she was yelling as she tangled and
wrestled to cornrow-braid her youngest
son's hair. He was two.

Pop… pop.

"Sit yo ass still!" she yelled again but this
time doing so while snatching a hand full of
hair to the left and staring down at him over
his right shoulder.

He was a tough one and in their *terrible
twos* they usually were. For some reason *this*
particular one on *this* particular day refused
to obey or cry. Oh yeah… he was crying,
but silently.

3

Tears were streaming down the young boy's face but no audible sound came with them. During his short life he had been through this routine several times. His only problem now was that he was itching to break away from his mama's death grip so that he, too, could become a part of that noise-making trio in the other room that was so steadily growing into the nuisance that was getting *his* head yanked and *his* ass spanked.

But even at two years old little Shemar could sense that something more than a lil ol' head of hair was bothering his mother. It had to be something a whole lot bigger than him.

Precious was dealing with and going through "*baby daddy drama*" again. It was always something. Every week.

To her each month was always full of either lies, late child *help* payments (because they sure as hell wasn't supporting anything), or bullshit.

Four kids… Four weeks… Four *baby daddies.* It all equaled out to *four* arguments per month.

"Girl, that nigga ain't going outta town this weekend. He just don't wanna keep his damn son," she said sounding frustrated as she spoke into the cell phone that was propped into the crook of her neck.

4

She listened as whoever on the other end spoke back before speaking again.

"Yeah… his ass got money to go outta town but he talkin' bout I'm trippin'. We'll see who's trippin' when I put his ass on child support fa real this time."

She snapped, "Shemar!" *pop… pop…* " I said sit--yo--ass--still!" Little Shemar got popped between every syllable.

"So what is your new boyfriend gonna say when he finds out that one of your kid's father left you…" the person paused to choose their words more wisely, "not wanting to sound--um, disrespectful but holding the bag this weekend?"

"What do you mean?" Precious asked.

"Well, ain't you and your man supposed to have something special planned for the two of ya'll to be alone this weekend?"

"*Hell naw, girl.* I'm just trying to hit the club tonight. *Shittt*, I ain't got no man."

And they both burst into laughter.

Don't want no man… Don't need no man…
Ain't got no man

Chapter Two

Paula was knee deep in reports. It was a Friday. The office's atmosphere was jovial and full of laughter and people were trying to get out of there. Approaching 3 o' clock, the company's official *let's go crazy* hour and mile mark where everyone loses their minds and will to work and collectively herd toward the time clock to punch out, Paula still found herself busy. *Real busy.*

"Still trying to figure out the nation's deficit?" one of her colleagues jokingly asked while briefly stopping by and sticking her head into Paula's office.

Paula was the boss…the manager, and everything rested upon her shoulders just as it had been for the last three years.

Thirty two years old… degreed and professional… no kids… and not only single, but *super* single.

"If Michelle and Barack can't do it," she began finally speaking on her friend's comment, "then I guess it would be left up to lil ol' me to fix."

The two of them laughed as Paula waved and watched her office-mate of six years turn and walk away to catch up with those who were already on their way out.

"See you Monday!" she heard the girl call out. And then the girl was gone.

Paula pushed away from her desk and reclined back in her chair as far as it had let her and took a breather. She wasn't bored. Nor tired. Nor defeated by any of the tasks at hand. She was...well, to tell the truth--she didn't know *what* the hell she was. She was a superwoman she knew, but by what means and by what measurements were she determining this she had no idea.

By no means was she ready for children and especially children out of wedlock. She had also prided herself in not being one to get pregnant before getting a diploma or a degree or at not letting a man get all up in the middle of her *business* before she even had a chance to start up a business. When times came when she did need a man up in the middle of her business (in which these times were far and few) she had no problem going to *"Wally World"* alone to purchase a pack or a box of condoms which would always be, for the most part, safe sex and for protection.

Now, although safe sex and protection from pregnancy was always first and foremost she'd still read the boxes and packaging labels in hopes of finding some sort of manu-facturer's enhanced cream or attached gadgetry that would also guaranty her of her own satisfying outcome during *and* by the end of these long awaited sexual encounters.

She had tried a variety of sorts.

She had tried ribbed, non-ribbed. Lubricated, non-lubricated. With and without spermicides. Thin, thinner, and super thin ones. Hell--she had even tried some fluorescent glow in the dark kinds. Each time she figured *"what the hell"*… after being one to wait so long for an in-between time to come when she could finally allow a man to *hit that* she'd be damned if she didn't get hers too…and hopefuly first.

Paula snapped out of her trance. The reports were still there beckoning her attention.

"Hello…," someone was saying from the doorway.

"Oh. Hi," Paula answered.

It was the guy whom was most whispered about around the water cooler.

"Wesley is it?" she added calling him by name.

"Yeah, but everybody around here calls me Wes."

The shortened-up nickname was thrown out there as an invite but Paula didn't bite. He was young, handsome, and as gossip had it... *fine* too. He was also intelligent, freshly hired, and from her standpoint probably planning to lure some non-suspecting upper management female into some major and very non-needed sex scandal and/or highly publicized sexual harassment case.

Whichever it was Paula stood strong with a definite *"no way, Jose... not here,"* she thought to herself feeling and sensing the game that was written all over this guy's cute ass face.

"It's a Friday," she reminded him, "why haven't you left like the rest of the crowd?"

"Well, honestly...I was hoping that you'd okay me for some overtime today. I just wanted to wait until everyone else was already gone before I asked."

Paula could smell a hint of nice smelling cologne stealing its way into her office and flirting with her all the way from where Wesley was standing. She thought about his request as she looked around her office. There were files and boxes of files everywhere. Although she wanted to tell the guy *"no"* reality was making a strong and convincing difference. Truth be told, she needed the help.

"I'll tell you what…," she began," give me fifteen minutes to run to the break room to get a soda and then you can meet me back here."

Before she could raise herself from her chair and get around her desk the good '*mister*' here surprised her and hit her with something different.

"How about allowing me to be the gentleman that my mother raised me to be and letting me to treat?" he offered. "I can go get the sodas and you--well, you just sit back and relax until I get back. You know…kind of like letting your second wind kick in."

"Nice gesture," Paula thought to herself but still didn't go for it.

She smiled.

"Kind of like giving back to the community ain't it, Wesley? I'll tell you what…save your money big spender. Overtime's not that easy to come by these days. I'll be back in fifteen."

And she left.

The smile that had appeared upon ol' Wes' face exposing all those perfect teeth never actually left but behind the mask his ego must've suffered a slight bruising. Nonetheless, if it did, he didn't allow it to show. He was cool.

Later after she had returned

"You're a workaholic, aren't you?" Wesley asked scooping up a stack of files from a nearby chair. He handed them to her. "No," Paula answered, "just doing me. I've got a job to do."

"And you do it well," he added with the possibility of the statement being borderline flirty.

Paula didn't allow Wesley's little *slick* comment to slide by without acknowledging it. She checked him. Quickly and politely. "Flattery won't get you anywhere, Wesley," she stated.

With an added air of professionalism she added, "but *that* kind of flattery *will* get your overtime cut short, if not also the tenure of your job."

Ouch now that hurt. But can't fault a man for trying. So after that the following two hours went by smoothly and as Paula had hoped in the beginning...strictly business.

The Drive Home

"The nerve of that brother trying to come on to me with all that *Denzel* mess," she was saying to herself.

"Hmph… '*and you do it well*'," she repeated remembering what Wes had said to set her off. She didn't allow it to show at the office but she seemed pretty ticked off about it now.

If Paula could hear herself and what she was saying she would've been surprised. The woman actually sounded mad especially considering the fact that she was talking to herself aloud.

Her thoughts kept coming and by the time that she was pulling her year old BMW into the garage of her neat and well-furnished condo she was furious.

The slamming of her car door could be heard over the low humming sound of the garage door now lowering itself back into place. Her keys jingled as she stepped toward the rear of the car. She reached into her backseat to retrieve her computer bag and then slammed *that* door before heading inside. Once inside after the keys hit the granite counter top and after the shoes came off to hit the center of the nicely tiled kitchen floor Paula snatched opened the door to her refrigerator and grabbed a bottled water.

She wanted to slam its door close but thought about all the items racked up on the inside of it. So to avoid having to clean up a mess later she slowly swung the door shut, turned around and leaned back against it. Sipping on the chilled water and still leaning back against the refrigerator Paula stood there just staring around herself and at her place.

"Ain't nothing wrong with me!" she exclaimed but not being exactly sure about the reason of her anger at the time or in the first place.

And who was she talking to? And who was she trying to convince?

She began walking through the quietness of her home toward her bedroom.

"I mean… I've got my own mortgage, my *own* money. I pay my own *luxury* car note, and I got real diamonds. I don't care how small they might be…they're real and they're mine."

Paula kept rattling.

"And nice clothes that I buy from real department stores and not from some jacked up hood spot with a rack full of knockoffs. *And* I've got me," she ended.

"So what the hell else do I need?" she asked herself.

Paula sat upon her bed but heard nothing. There was no one there to answer her. She had become just as digitalized and self-sufficient as everything else that she had bought and surrounded herself with.

There was a clock that sat upon her bedside nightstand that was the kind that had a little lense on top that would shoot a beam of light up to the ceiling to illuminate the time of day or night. A person didn't even have to roll over to check for time…just open your eyes and there it was. It just hung there like some kind of electronic moon or something.

But she began thinking about the clock in different terms now.

Never had it ever stared back at her… Never had it looked her in her eyes… and NEVER had it ever whispered to her those three words of endearment that every woman loves to hear. Not the '*I love you*', but the other three, '*I'm fitna cum!*'.

Her frustration grew…or maybe it was just her hormones. They had been acting up a little lately.

Paula fell back into her bed and closed her eyes. When she opened them again she noticed that silent ass clock gleaming its presence back down at her from the ceiling again.

It pissed her off.

"Screw you!" she shouted and with a certain validity in her voice she added, "I don't *need* no man!"

Don't want no man... Don't need no man...
Ain't got no man

Chapter Three

Jojo was just itching for an opportunity to call Precious back but if not that at least a phone call *from* Precious would've been cool.

It was a boring Friday night and there was nothing to do.

8: 30 came... nothing

9:15 came... still no call

At 10 o' clock Precious' phone rung. It allowed her favorite ringtone of the month to entertain her as she grabbed it up to check the caller ID. Slightly disappointed at it not being her son's father she answered.

"Hello."

"You ain't gone yet?" Jojo asked.

"Nope," Precious answered looking over at Shemar who for some reason was still wide awake and still full of energy.

"Baby daddy number four must haven't showed yet?"

"Naw--and he ain't gonna show," Precious snapped. "Man… that fool don't care nothing 'bout his son!"

Jojo relaxed and listened as Precious began venting, and though they had been struggling with an idea to do something to change the mode they figured that it was probably best to allow Precious to get some things off her chest before finally running it by her.

"Hey--how about me coming by to scoop you and your son up and taking you both out to eat somewhere? It'll be on me. My treat."
Precious thought about it. Shemar was still up and all of her other kid's dads had picked her other kids up and of course… it *was* a Friday night.
Precious may have been lonely and bored but she damn sure wasn't no fool.
"How long?" she asked.
Jojo answered, "an hour… give me time to shower and to slide on some jeans and I'll be there."
There were a couple of goodbyes and the line went dead.

Precious' outfit of what she had planned on wearing to the club, if she had went, had already been laid-out earlier so she figured to hell with trying to put something else together.

"I might as well go ahead and still wear this," she concluded which was a good thing because after getting herself dressed it would still take all of thirty minutes to wrestle and put up with little Shemar to get him ready to go.

An hour or so later

Precious opened her front door at Jojo's third knock. Before she could actually greet Jojo there was a noise that came from behind her.

"Boy!" she screamed looking back over her shoulder, "leave that mess alone and c'mon!"

Her attention had been drawn toward Shemar who while playing with his little *HotWheels* cars on her coffee table had knocked something over so that when the door opened revealing her in her outfit she never saw the look that had come across Jojo's face.

It was shocking.

"Damn," Jojo thought aloud, "you look good as a…"

Precious' head spun back around giving her the opportunity to take in the sight of Jojo which surprised her.

"And you look--comfortable," she complimented though now feeling slightly overdressed.

Jojo's attire wasn't only just very comfortable looking, it was *really really* casual too.

The hair was perfect and even the shirt was actually nice. But the jeans…well, the jeans--they seemed to almost sag or something. It was like they were hanging a little *too* low off of Jojo's waistline.

Precious didn't trip though. Hell, if Jojo wanted to dress like that who was she to judge them for what they wore. Even *her* dress code and some of her club outfits could be questionable at times. In fact, Precious was wearing one of those outfits tonight.

Jojo drove and together they talked, joked and laughed about almost everything as Shemar surprisingly rode in silence. He would look at the two of them occasionally but for the most part he just stared out the window and smiled the whole time. Little Shemar probably knew that by the way everyone was smiling and talking that they were more than likely going somewhere special. And that meant...

Translation: Somewhere where he probably had enough space to really run around and act a damn fool. And in that case, he was being smart enough to save his energy.

The atmosphere of the restaurant was cool and laid-back.

Precious was so glad that Jojo had actually offered to pay for the nightout because by the look of things... the food prices, drink prices, games and all the other bells and whistles, this would've hit her pockets pretty hard and definitely would've set her back a little.

They were seated at a table.

Although Shemar was still in 'best behavior' mode you could tell that the little son-of-a-gun was gearing himself up to be ready for takeoff. His eyes were taking in all the sights and darting every which-a-way. Precious was proud of him thus far because the last thing that she wanted right now was for him to embarrass here in public *or* in front of her friend.

"What do you want to drink?" Jojo asked.
"I want a frozen margarita," Precious answered with no hesitation.
Jojo looked toward the little one,"*and what about him?*"
"I'll just order him an orange juice or something."
A waitress finally came around and their initial order was taken. Added to it was a large basket of French fries just for starters.
Jojo beginning approach was with a simple conversation.
"I'm glad that you're not still as mad as you were when I was talking to you earlier."
"Yeah... well-- I'm cool now," Precious answered looking around and hoping that the waitress would hurry back with their drinks. She loved margaritas.
"If it ain't one of them niggas tripping over one thing then it's always another one tripping over something else. Trust and believe that it's always something. Shit--you know how niggas are."
They both laughed as Jojo looked and took note at the way Precious' right eye kind of squinted as she did. For a split second Precious noticed that stare from Jojo. She

21

had noticed that look before but quickly blew it off.

"I've had people look at me like that," she told herself, "but maybe I'm just tripping."

The drinks came. The waitress apologized for the long wait and then with a smile assured them that their fries were almost done and would be out shortly.

"Okay, that's cool. Thanks sweetie," Jojo told the waitress which was something else that Precious had picked up on and casually blew off... *again.*

Eight minutes later the fries arrived and as everyone dug in, even little Shamar with a fry in each hand, the waitress stood by with patience allowing everybody to get those first couple of mouthfuls over with that usually calms the *hungries* so that she could take the rest of their orders for their main courses.

Surprisingly Jojo ordered for everyone.

Precious listened in kinda feeling awkward about how Jojo had took the initiative in getting a clear understanding on what she and Shemar had wanted to eat before actually conveying that order to *Alicia*, which was what the waitress' name tag read.

"Hmph... that's weird," Precious acknowledged to herself looking at things a little more closely now. "That's how all my baby daddies used to do. Order for everybody else."

The ordering was done and the waitress shot off to go wherever they went to do what they needed to do to get their patrons order put in and their foods back to them.

"You wanna go play games, lil man?" Jojo asked Shemar and then looked at Precious before adding, "I mean… if that's cool with you… You can stay here and enjoy the rest of your drink."

Precious gave Jojo the "OK" and they left.

Watching the two as they began fading off into the crowd Precious leisurely began observing Jojo's 'everything' all over again. Slowly she began noticing some things about Jojo that she obviously had been missing at first.

But how could she?

How could she have missed these things she asked herself now. She had tried telling herself *again* that maybe she was just tripping… and that the margarita that she was sipping on was just a little too strong.

Precious sipped again… and again… and again as she waited for Jojo and Shemar to return during which time now she used to recount the moment and day that she and Jojo had actually met and to recall each and every conversation that they had ever had since.

Dollar store...Toy isle...Jojo was stocking... Kids were all over the place and running Precious crazy. Noise and yells were coming from two or three different directions "Mama I want this!" and "Mama can I have this?". Even little Shemar was doing his share at grabbing at everything. All of this was happening in the midst of another child "help" payment when...
    "Excuse me..." the stock girl had said stepping up to her, "but do you mind if I asked you where you get your hair done? I like that."
    Precious told her and that struck up a couple of laughs. They exchanged phone numbers and eventually things evolved to the conversation that they were having earlier today as Precious struggled to braid Shemar's hair.
    But somehow she had missed it. Precious just didn't see it coming... not until now.
    Still she hoped that she was wrong.

Here they come.

She hid her thoughts as they were approaching but her eyes stayed constantly and trained on Jojo.

Jojo and Shemar were all smiles so Precious talent-ly did her part joining in and smiled with them pretending not to actually notice Jojo's swag now…a swag that was a lot more masculine tonight than she had picked up on before.

Stunned she took a big sip of the margarita--a *big long* sip of margarita. With the strong drink still stuck in her throat it hit her.

"Oh My God…" she whispered to herself, "this *bitch* is gay."

Don't want no man... Don't need no man...
Ain't got no man

Chapter Four

It was morning again and Precious woke up in bed alone, except for her son.

It was his stirring that had done it.

She stumbled out of her bed and went into the bathroom. After relieving herself she went back to the room, got Shemar and got their teethes brushed and faces washed and then headed to the kitchen.

They ate.

It was quiet, peaceful, and relaxing.

There were no extra noises from any of her 8, 6 or 4 year old's screams. No cries. No complaints about what they did or *didn't* want to eat this morning or tattle-telling on who was doing what to whom.

In the distant she heard her cellphone. It was the first call of the day.

The phone was in her bedroom so she rushed to get it.

"Damn, who is this calling me so early on a Saturday morning?"

Grabbing her cell phone and heading back into the kitchen she answered, "Hello?"

"Hey, sleepyhead... are you up yet?" the familiar voice asked.

Damn, Precious had forgotten to look at the caller ID.

It was her... him... shit, she didn't know what to say. Precious was confused and didn't want to label anyone. She wasn't the judgmental type but this just wasn't her thing. With no pun intended she just went for it.

"Yeah, girl--," she started, "um, Jojo. I'm up."

Precious felt weird about catching or trying to correct herself but hell Jojo hadn't said anything yet about being called girl... or *man*, so why trip now?

But it wasn't Jojo it was Precious who was tripping. Jojo hadn't said a thing... not even last night. Jojo was cool and had acted solely as a friend. Someone who knew Precious' situation and empathized with her. Someone who supported her.

Precious checked her emotions and continued on with the conversation.

"What's got you up so early?" she asked Jojo.

"Early? Sweetie, it's almost noon."

Precious couldn't help to think. "Damn... there she go with that 'Sweetie' shit again".

27

"Noon? Hell, I thought it was still around 10 o'clock. Where you at?" Precious asked still trying to be a friend and still appreciative for last night.

"At work. Im on break," Jojo answered.

"Oh. Okay."

Precious waited as a strange silence fell between the two.

"Umm, look…" she started.

"Precious," Jojo interrupted. "I kind of already know what you're thinking and what you're probably about to say."

Nothing was said but as Jojo was about to continue Precious snapped out of it.

"Jojo," Precious sighed, "when I mentioned to you yesterday about me not having a man… it didn't mean," she paused. "Well-- shit, Jojo it didn't mean that I wasn't *strictly dickly*… kno' what I mean?" she asked being straight forward. It was more like a confession.

"Yeah I know what you mean, girl. But you tripping. I ain't trying to force myself on you. I mean you're cute and all--hell, even sexy too… *real* sexy," she joked, "but in reality I just saw a sistah struggling.I felt your pain and just wanted to help you out."

Jojo ended it with that and waited for what she had said to settle. Precious felt like shit

28

and was embarrassed. She searched for words but couldn't find any.

"Shit," she said cursing herself aloud.

"I take that as an apology?" Jojo joked.

"Yeah well. I guess I do owe you one."

"Then say it," Jojo pushed.

"Say what?" Precious asked now finally cracking a smile.

"Tell me that you're sorry."

"Sorry for what?" she asked with a hint of pride in her voice.

"Sorry for thinking that you were '*all that*' and for thinking that all I wanted to do was to get in your panties."

"I don't wear panties," Precious joked. She immediately regretted it the moment it slipped from her lips.

"Ohh… okay. You wanna play with fire?" Jojo asked reminding her of her leopard spots. Jojo wasn't about to change her ways just because Precious didn't get down like that.

"Naw. My bad. But look… I am sorry for jumping the gun and I *did* enjoy and appreciate last night. You forgive me?" she asked.

"Yeah, I ain't tripping. But what are you going to do about these men problems you have?"

"Men problems that I have? What are you going to do about yours?" Precious shot back.

"Mine? Don't get it twisted, baby," Jojo informed her. " I might be too much woman for you-- but I *damn sho'* don't want no man."

Together as they laughed the ice begin to break.

Don't want no man… Don't need no man…
Ain't got no man

Chapter Five

Monday morning came around and Paula's office was neat again. So much so now that it had actually surprised her when she stepped in herself. She had forgotten what an organized office even looked like.

Hell, it had been just that long.

Sitting in her chair now and getting situated behind her desk she closed her eyes. This was a new practice of hers that she had begin. Meditation she had called it and because she couldn't think of any kind of yoga mantra or something to chant, like Russell Simmons probably did each morning before he got started, she instead went with her next best possible choice… *his brother*. Ron.

"Who's house?" she chanted.

Breathe out… Breathe in…

"Who's house?" again she chanted still with her eyes closed.

Before she got a chance to breathe either out or in someone ruined it for her.

"Ron's house," she heard.

It came from the doorway.

Surprisingly it was the receptionist that ran the front office area of the company. She was a little small-framed cute white girl.

"And what do *you* know about that?" Paula asked.

"Oh, because I'm white I'm not supposed to know about rap? Or RUN-DMC?" the girl asked.

"Well-- I wasn't talking about your whiteness... In actuality, I was talking about your *youthfulness*... girl, you are way too young to know about them," Paula told her with a smile.

A light and sociably-correct interoffice giggle and laugh was shared between the two as the receptionist stretched out her arms and held out something... it was a floral arrangement.

"Flowers?" Paula asked, "For who?"

"For you I guess. That's what the delivery guy said when he dropped them off. Aren't they pretty?" she added as she walked and placed the vase on Paula's desk.

Paula looked up at her with a puzzled look and then back to the flowers. Nothing was said.

"Well?" the front office girl finally asked.

"Well what?" Paula questioned searching her mind for her own answers.

"Well, are they from a new spark or an old flame?"

"A new spark?"

Paula definitely didn't want to go there.

The receptionist gave her that '*you know what I mean*' look.

"Hey--don't you have a job that needs to be tended to that's somehow being neglected right now?" Paula joked.

Another office laugh between the two and the front office girl took off leaving her boss alone with the floral arrangement.

Paula looked at the flowers.

"Pretty," she said now reaching inside the small envelope to tug the card out. It read:

Please accept each petal, leaf, bloom, or blossom from me as a token of my apology for all that any of them may have done to hurt you.

Sincerely,

And that was it.

"What the hell…"

Paula's face had an even worse look of confusion upon it. She turned the card over but still nothing. There was no signature. No initials. No nothing. Not anything that could've told her something or given her a hint as to who they may have come from. She gave the vase of flowers a spin and looked them over once more.

"Now who on earth would be sending me these?" she asked herself … still she came up zilch…nada…nothing.

She hadn't slept with anyone lately so that wasn't it. Neither had there been any new, as the receptionist had put it, *sparks* generating in her furnace. The process of elimination became torture but Paula had work to do. She couldn't just spend her day worrying about some flowers that may have arrived accidently to the wrong person or whatever.

She slid the vase over to a recently emptied spot on her desk and began her day.

Five minutes til lunch

Knock…Knock…Knock…

It was Paula's officemate of six years again.

"Whoa… nice flowers," she said. "Looks like somebody's been playing in the sandbox."

"I beg your pardon. Girl, quit it," Paula said to her friend and co-worker. "And regardless… if I *had* been playing in the sandbox, as you so eloquently put it, wouldn't that be my business and very inappropriate for me to be discussing here at the office?"

34

"Well, I'd tell you if I got sand in my panties," the friend admitted.

"Really? Girl, now that really would be *TMI*," Paula answered still sharing a laugh with her.

"Whatever," she responded walking over to Paula's desk and bending down, "mmm... smell good."

"Yeah, they do don't they?" Paula agreed while still actually trying to mentally count back to the time when she *had* gotten some sand in her panties... *sex* wise.

She was in a zone.

Her co-worker's question snapped her out of it.

"Who are they from?" she asked.

"Your guess is as good as mine," Paula answered pulling the note from its envelope once more as they both begin reading it together.

"Romantic...and apologetic," Paula said trying to figure a way to put things.

"And bullshit!" her friend added.

"If he meant it he would've signed it, Paula!"

"Good point," Paula agreed tucking the card back into its small envelope.

Her co-worker's comment concluded the conversation and the topic was dead. Paula got her things together and shut her computer down. "I'm ready to eat," she said leading the way out her office.

The two women enjoyed their lunch together without once speaking another word about the mysterious vase of flowers or the note.

As they were leaving the break room... out of nowhere someone opened and held the door for them.

"Allow me," Wes said. His smile was beaming.

"Aren't you the perfect gentleman," Paula's friend told him.

"Well, I'm just trying to make up for all of the ones out there that's not."

When he said this he looked straight at Paula and that's when it hit her... the flowers. It hit her and it took her by surprise.Though her co-worker didn't seem to catch on Paula noticed a very suspicious and deliberate smile that Wesley had shot at her.

He knew about the flowers. He was guilty and he knew it. Wesley had to have been the one who had sent them. Paula sensed it and her gut instincts convinced her as well. It was something about his look. About what he had said, what the card had said...everything. It was just too much.

Paula wasn't some type of private investigator or nothing like that but she sure as hell didn't need a freaking map to connect all the damn dots on this one either.

Case closed. It was him!

She rolled her eyes .

"I should fire his ass!" she thought to herself.

Paula held her anger until she and her co-worker had split up and until after she could make it back to her office and shut her door.

Why--she couldn't just fire the man!

Hell, on what grounds? What had he done against Company Policy? *Nothing*...that she could prove.

What about his work ethics... performance? No complaints there either. Wes had been smart enough to *not* sign the card that the flowers had came with which now could totally leave him anonymous and in the clear.

"Just in case I wanted to fire his ass!" Paula thought to herself.

She fumed.

Paula was still staring at the intrusive vase of flowers on her desk when someone began knocking at her office door.

"Come in," she said.

It was Jayla... one of her department supervisors.

"Hey Paula... you got a minute?" the woman asked sticking her head in.

"Sure. Come on in," Paula answered while doing a quick transformation back to pro-corporate mode, "whatcha got?"

Jayla stepped in.

"Well, to start with..." she stopped abruptly, "dang--who cleaned up *this* office?"

"Oh--you like?" Paula asked spreading her arms like...*behold.*

It looks better," Jayla told her.

"Yeah, I know...thanks. Now what's up with the sit down?" Paula asked.

"Well, just to get straight to the point. Paula, my numbers are falling behind because my department is still one clerk short. I really need someone else. Can I *please* hire someone?"

"Have you pulled and looked at any apps from HR yet?"

"Actually I'm a step ahead of you," Jayla said her pulling out sheets of paper from a folder.

"Look..." she began pointing out names as she went, "I've got these three girls that I've checked out--one that I really like. I wanna call this one back in for a second interview.

However, before I did I wanted to see what you thought about it and to get your *okay*".

Paula took the three applications that were handed to her and looked them over.

"Which one you want to hire?" she asked again though trust-ing Jayla's judgment.

"Josilyn Hatcher... look at her app. Stable job history, diploma, some college, no felonies or criminal history, she's computer literate...I think we can work with her."

Paula handed the papers back to her, "Okay. Approved. Get it done," she told her.

As Jayla was leaving Paula stopped her.

"Um--Jayla, isn't that guy Wesley Cox in your department?"

"Yeah--Wes? He's in my group. Why, is something wrong?"

Paula began thinking about how she should approach the situation... or even *if* she should approach the situation at all.

She played it off... kept it work related.

"No. Nothing's wrong," she responded. "I was just thinking about those other applications. Is he pulling his weight and getting his numbers? Or is all the attention from him being the only man or *decent* looking man over there distracting him?"

Paula paused to choose her next words wisely.

"I mean--do we need to reconsider his employment with us? We could try making some room for one of those other qualified girls in your stack there to insure your team's numbers."

She didn't know exactly how it had sounded or came out but she did decide to just stop while she was ahead. Jayla looked at her for a second. Paula was afraid that she may have said the wrong thing and by the way that she was being looked at it made her nervous.

It was a puzzled look that came from the Wes' supervisor. She didn't exactly know how to tell her boss what she needed to tell her but she still took a shot at it.

Jayla stepped back into Paula's office and closed the door.

"Paula, not only are Wes' numbers higher than anyone else's numbers over there, but ultimately *he* was the one who had pulled us through with our numbers last month. But that's not all. I'm the one that hired him, Paula. And…"

"And what…?" Paula asked compelling Jayla to continue.

"And--I hired him because I felt sorry for him."

"What!" Paula exclaimed. "Felt sorry for him? Jayla, this isn't some charitably based company. We *hire* for jobs… we do not *give* them away."

Paula felt her blood pressure rising.

"I know, Paula. But please listen…the man has had it hard."

Jayla began explaining.

"First, he came home from the military only to discover that his *Baby Mama* was strung out on drugs. The girl was selling all of her food stamps and trading them for drugs and stuff…and she *kept* the kid filthy. After fighting and going through court dates and all that and finally winning and getting custody of his daughter--the mans's mama died."

"What? Damn…" Paula mustered out.

"Yep. Damn is right," Jayla agreed, " I gave him the job three days after he buried his mother."

Don't want no man… Don't need no man…
Ain't got no man

Chapter Six

"I got another job!" Jojo was yelling through the phone.

"Another job?" Precious asked, "what other job?"

Jojo told her.

At first she hadn't wanted to say anything about it until she had gotten the word that she was hired and had known for sure. It hadn't been ten minutes passed from the time that she had had her second interview for a job that she had applied for well over a month before. Afterwards she couldn't wait to call Precious.

"They just called me up out of the blue yesterday and asked me to come in for a second interview with the head lady," she was saying.

"That's good," Precious told her, "congratulations."

"Thank ya. Im happy…. what are you doing?"

"Watching my kids and about to wash one of my daughter's hair."

"You want some company?"

Precious had cleared the air with Jojo by making it specifically understood that she didn't go that way. And although Jojo had said it was cool… Precious *still* wasn't comfortable enough yet to have Jojo over as a '*chillin out*' type of guest. Not tonight…and probably not ever.

"Not tonight, Jo," she simply told her, "maybe some other time--the kids are…" "The kids are what, Precious? At home…sleep…in your bed? Hey, you know what… I ain't even tripping. It's like you said, boo. *Humph*… maybe some other time."

Jojo hung up. After that Precious froze knowing that she had offended Jojo and possibly hurt her feelings.

"Damn!" she cried out, "why do I always get mixed up in all the crazy mess?"

But she knew the answer. She was just too damn kind.

At twenty-four with four kids she hadn't been able to tell a man '*no*' since she was sixteen years old and now here she was all alone, no job, no education, no hustle and still finding it hard to say it…but this time to a woman.

"Well *no*. *Unh-Unh*, Miss Jojo. You ain't getting none of this," she proclaimed feeling like she had just made another New Year's resolution.

Problem was…she aint never kept one.

Don't want no man… Don't need no man…
Ain't got no man

Chapter Seven

Josilyn "Jojo" Hatcher reported to her
new job two weeks after the day that she had
learned that she was hired. To train her Jayla
had put her best man on the job… literally.

Wes accepted the responsibility that fell
into his lap with gladness and it turned out
to be a good thing because unlike Precious,
Jayla had recognized her new clerk's swag
right off the bat making it an easy judgment
call to couple the two.

In doing so she killed two birds with one
stone.

Josilyn wouldn't go after Wes because she
didn't do men and Wes wouldn't go after
Josilyn because… *well, you know the rest.*

Everyone would be happy…well,
everyone except for Paula.

She had been torturing herself and kicking
her own butt be-hind her being insensitive
toward a man who was only trying to put in
a few more hours a week at work in order to
care for his kid.

"Shame on me," she had told herself while at times being filled with so much self-embarrassment that she would even swear. "Damn!"

But how could she make up for it?
How could she help him with something other than just overtime?
She had even been rude to him and threatened the man's job so how could she even apologize to him if it came down to it for that?

Paula had been entertaining these questions over and over again during the last two weeks that had passed while also doing her best to avoid Wes (which at times was very difficult).
It was a given that eventually she'd have to walk the floor because it was her job to periodically do that. And because it was her job to do so and she'd have to do it soon instead of staying all cooped-up in her office waiting on the shame to wear off or until she could figure out what to do.
She had remembered what her mother had told her many years earlier about being embarrassed to apologize for something that you've done wrong… *"Baby," her mom tell*

her, *" you can't save your face and your ass at the same damn time."*

And Mama was right. Paula had no plans on being fired, she had bills to pay. So one day after she had held her water for as long as she could and not being able to hold it any longer she left her office and jetted for the ladies room...fast.

It felt as if her bladder was about to explode.

Once relieved she decided to take a detour through the office in order to pick up a soda from the break room *and* to finally do that walk around that she had been neglecting.

Good idea... but it was very bad timing.

Wouldn't you know it 'cause just as she was approaching to go *in* the break room door at that exact same moment Wes was coming *out* of the break room door.

Yep, damn...their eyes met. And then...
BAM!!!

Without warning Wes let the door slam right in Paula's face.

It was *very* rude and *very* deliberate.

Paula didn't know that he could be so mean, but...

"So much for him being a gentleman," she thought to herself but still figured that she probably had it coming anyway.
So, whatever. She got her soda and headed back to her office.

47

No sooner than she had planted her butt back in her chair someone appeared in her door.

"Paula--may I speak with you?" the familiar voice said.

Paula's heart dropped, stopped, locked-up, skipped a beat, drained itself it seemed of all bodily fluids and almost left her lifeless. All this happened in a split-second's time before any one of her other valuable faculties could register or respond.

"Paula," Wes asked again allowing her name to hang in mid-air , "can I speak with you please?"

"Uh--yes,Wesley. Please... come in," she told him.

Wes walked in and closed the door behind himself.

Paula didn't know what to say.

Him being here was one thing. Her knowing what to do now that he *was* here was another. Things were already awkward enough due to what had just occurred at the break room. But now here he was just standing here not saying anything.

Wes hadn't spoken not one single word.

Paula's senses were still trying to catch up with what was happening in real life time when suddenly a piece of paper that Wes had been holding was being placed in front of her.

She looked down at it… then up, and then down again. She read it.

"What's this?"

"My two week's notice," he told her.

"Your two weeks' notice?"

Paula almost choked. Wes had shocked her and caught her off guard.

"You've found or gotten another job?" she asked.

"No," he answered, "but I can't afford to stay here. I have responsibilities. And…I'm embarrassed."

"Embarrassed? Embarrassed about what, Wesley?"

"Well," he said holding his head down, "my supervisor told me that you…".

Wes went silent.

Silence filled the room as Wes fought to find confidence to continue. He placed his hands over his face and with a wiping motion that looked as if he was attempting to remove every paragraph of pain that may have been written upon it, pulled them down heavily across his skin.

"You supervisor told you that I what?" Paula asked with confusion written upon her own face.

"That you had asked about me," he finished.

Paula remembered the conversation. But just how much had been told to him she wondered.

At the time she was not only careful with what she had revealed to Jayla but had remained professional about it as well. His *supervisor* shouldn't had taken it no further than that. But Paula, finally back in full pro mode again began taking control of the situation with a considerable view of the company's best interest.

Jayla had told her about Wesley's numbers.

"You're a great employee," Paula said to him. "I was only concerned about her department's overall performance *collectively*."

"But isn't it true that you hired that girl Jojo to replace me because you were mad at me?"

"*Mad* at you?" Paula asked. He surprised her, "mad at you about what?"

Wes came straight out with it...

"About Friday and some of the things that you felt that I had inappropriately said."

He paused and then added, "Or about the flowers that I had sent."

When he said it it was more like with an air of confidence rather than with conviction. Again Paula was taken aback. She took a breath. Wes had been standing the entire time.

"Wes," she began but afterwards took a long pause. Please--have a seat," she finally ended while using a hand gestured motion toward a chair on the other side of her desk.
Breathe out... Breathe in...
"*Who's house?*"
This was not happening, Paula wished for herself.
But it was… Right now… Live and in living color.
And again… *Breathe out... Breathe in…*
"*Paula's House!*" she said …actually almost *too* loud.
Wes thought that he had heard her say something.
"Excuse me?' he asked.

Don't want no man… Don't need no man…
Ain't got no man

Chapter Eight

A month or so later.
No one knew how *any* of it had happened.
Paula was sleeping with Wes.
Precious was sleeping with Jojo.
And everything else was going
progressively and smoothly.

It was a Thursday evening.
Paula had been letting Wes, what she was
nowadays calling him herself, get as much
OT that he could want or could handle.
She had yet to meet his daughter but had
been deciding that a slow approach would
probably be best for everyone. Still, he
never talked about her much nor offered to
bring her around. Paula didn't push.
"The two of them need time alone," she
figured thinking more of them rather than
just herself.

Though Paula had already left the office
for the day Wes had been left behind at
work to get more of his overtime done. She
could've stayed as well…there was always

something on her desk that was needing to be completed or signed off on but today she also needed to get some shopping done. They had been planning a date for the following night when after working late they'd leave together and share an intimate night of dinner and music at her place.

They had shared moments together before... *sexual* moments, but none that had lasted through the night or over night. Wes had always had to leave to get to his daughter.

"What's her name," Paula had asked him once.

"Uh...Tinker," he had answered.

"As in *Tinker Bell?*"

"Yeah...as in the fairy tale," he had concurred.

Tonight Paula found herself in a checkout line but in front of a woman with a lot less items in her basket than she.

"You can go ahead of me," Paula had told the lady.

The lady appeared to be middle aged or slightly older than Paula and quite energetic.

"Are you sure, honey?" the woman questioned staring down into her own basket.

All she had was ice cream, a magazine, and some batteries."

"Of course," Paula answered pulling her own basket aside and allowing the woman to pass.

A scary thought crossed Paula's mind... *this* was a lonely woman.

Paula recognized the traits. Sure the woman was cute and all...but ice cream, magazines, and BATTERIES!

Didn't take a rocket scientist.

The woman did one of those no-look quick peripheral scan of Paula's basket as she thanked her and exchanged places. Paula thought about her own items now...wine, ingredients for a salad, cheese, grapes, a few other personal items and "*shit*," Paula thought to herself... *a big ass box of condoms...ribbed!*

She felt her cheeks go flush. She was so for sure that the woman had spotted them.

"Oh well, at least I'm not the one using batteries tonight," Paula thought.

"Big date tonight?" the nosey woman asked.

Paula wanted to tell her '*none of your damn business*' but didn't.

She hadn't known if the woman was just being nice because of seeing the wine, the grapes, the cheese and stuff...or being *messy* as hell after seeing that damn box of rubbers that she had messed up and put where her loaf of bread should've been!

Paula cursed herself but smiled anyway.

"Somewhat," she answered quickly… fake smile still intact.

The woman then caught Paula staring at her batteries.

Well-- she didn't really *catch* Paula looking…Paula was *kinda* doing it on purpose. Woman's intuition was telling Paula that the woman was being a little out of line and that she *was* speaking on her condoms.

The woman then *somewhat* confessed by lowering her voice and leaned in to whisper to the woman now behind her as the checkout girl tallied up her total.

"Mine don't leave a mess, don't complain about my mother, and instead of putting him out my house every night--I just put 'em up in the top of my closet and gone on about my business."

"Now that was way Too Much Damn Information," Paula thought and before she could actually think of anything to say…

"Next…" the checkout girl said.

Paula watched as little *Miss Lonely* and *Nosey* trailed her happy ass on down the road.

55

"Look at her," Paula said to herself somehow mad at the woman now, "just itching to hurry up and get her ass home to use them batteries!"

Don't want no man… Don't need no man…
Ain't got no man

Chapter Nine

Precious couldn't believe it at first.
How could it have happened?
How *did* it happen?
Oh, she knew how it happened… she just
didn't know *how* it happened.

She and Jojo were laid up in each other's
arms one night as she began thinking back.
The first time that it happened Jojo had
asked her afterwards, "are you cool with
this?"
Precious had remained silent…partly
because she didn't know what to say, but
moreso because she was still out of breath.
She was out of breath, speechless and still
trying to regain control of her legs. But by
the time that they had stopped quivering,
trembling and shaking--Jojo was back
between them.
Lucky for Jojo *that* night all four of the
children's fathers had come through.
Precious and Jojo had been alone then.

But they weren't tonight. The kids were
asleep. They hadn't made-out but after

putting all the kids to bed they were at least spending quality time together. Even little Shemar had called it a night.

So many thoughts filled Precious' head. She still wasn't allowing herself to be getting all mushy with Jojo in front of the kids but still... *this.*

"How did it get to this?" she wondered.

Jojo squeezed her a bit tighter and kissed her.

"What are you thinking about?" she asked Precious.

"You."

"What about me?"

"Well... how sweet you are to me and how kind you are to my kids," she answered. And then she added, "you know--all the things that I had hoped for in their daddies."

Precious didn't know it but although she hadn't meant any harm in what she had said Jojo had somehow read in between the lines and received it differently.

She translated it to: "*I done had so many 'bad' men in my life that ain't done shit for me that I might as well get a 'good' woman that will.*"

Jojo smiled and gave Precious another kiss.

"So you're saying that I'm everything to you that them other nigga supposed to had been. Right?"

"Nooo," Precious lied, "I didn't mean it like that. I'm just saying that you came in the game and played it right. I'm the one that's a rookie."

They began laughing. Precious climbed up and straddled Jojo's body and began kissing her.

"You know that you can't spend the night, don't you? It won't be long before one of my kids wake up and come crying at my door wanting to come get in the bed with me."

"Yeah, I know. I've got to go home and get ready for work tomorrow anyway."

They both got up.

As they were walking to the door Precious asked Jojo, "how's the new job working out?"

"It's cool. Better money, no weekends, not a lot of standing or walking around either. I like it."

"You still training with that guy?"

Jojo stopped and thought about Wes.

"You know…" she started, "he's cool and everything. But it's something *different* about that dude."

"Different? Precious asked. "Different as in *gay*?"

"Naw, naw…not like that. Different as in *shiesty*. I don't trust him. It's something about his swag… it's like--it's fake."

Jojo turned around at the door kissed her new girlfriend and left.

Precious closed the door and spun around in time enough to see her oldest son standing at the corner of the hallway wiping sleep from his eyes.

It scared her… not his presence, but the thought of if he had saw anything.

Her heart jumped.

"Hey, baby. What's wrong? You can't sleep?"

The boy was still shaking his head from side to side as she took his hand and led him into her room. They both climbed into her bed. The faint smell of Jojo's body scent still lingered on her pillow as she laid hugging her son and allowing her future man of the house to fall back asleep.

Before falling asleep herself Precious thought… "*For many years though I've done my thing at will I've done it with respect to my kids and never allowed them to see a lot of men running in and out of my life or my home… I damn sho' not about to*

start now--especially with no freaking
woman!!"

She had made it up in her mind then that she'd have to have a talk with Jojo. This had went too far. Precious would have to end it... NOW!

Don't want no man… Don't need no man…
Ain't got no man

Chapter Ten

Friday's workday was blowing by fast
and 5 o'clock was approaching even
quicker.

And it was a payday.

The checks had been passed out and all of
the *let's go crazy attitudes* had already
begun spreading.

Jojo had waited until lunch to call Precious
to tell her about her … a check that was
going to be a "free" check for Jojo. Luckily
she was caught up with her bills because the
dang thing just happened to be short.

"How short is it?" Precious asked.

"Just a couple of days," Jojo answered.
"My supervisor is gone for the rest of the
day but I'm gonna show it to her boss after
lunch."

"Am I going to see you tonight?" Precious
asked, "I need to talk to you."

"Yeah… I'll be over there early. I wanna
do something nice for you and all the kids."

The conversation ended shortly after that.
Jojo hung up the phone and finished her
lunch. After leaving the break room she
remembered how many times she had seen

her supervisor's boss still in her office working during lunch. This was after everyone else had left. It was the same woman whom she had had her second interview with… "Paula was it?" she asked herself.

Maybe the woman had skipped lunch today too. Jojo hoped that she was there so she wouldn't have to wait until afterwards.

"Might as well," she told herself and headed that way.

It was an office space full of cubicles. However after rounding the last corner from the direction that she had come she could see directly into Paula's office.. *and* she could see what was happening in Paula's office.

But they didn't see her… or maybe it was just the fact that they were too busy doing what they were doing that they *couldn't* see her.

"Damn," Jojo said stopping dead in her tracks.

She took a few steps backwards. She was sure that she hadn't been seen… but *dammnn.* Jojo couldn't believe what she had saw. She turned to go.

But…

"Shit! You scared me," Jojo said startled.

Jojo had bumped into someone who was coming up behind her.

"What the hell are you doing?" the woman asked.

She had appeared out of nowhere.

Jojo thought fast of something to say.

"I--um, I forgot something in the break room. I was turning around to go get it."

"Well, baby be careful. And people usually don't walk backwards to *turn* around," the woman sternly said and warned before stepping around Jojo and walking off.

"Shit," Jojo said again now heading down the hallway. "And where the fuck did she come from?"

Jojo had seen the woman around before but didn't actually know her nor what department she worked in. Her mind searched… it was weird. It almost seemed as if the woman was sneaking up on *her*. She continued her mental search.

"Damn, what department have I seen her in?"

And then it hit her.

It hadn't been a *department* that she had seen the woman in, it was in the break room—with Paula. This was the lady that when Paula did take out the time to do lunch, she did it with her.

But was the woman watching me? And didn't it seem like she had an attitude?

Something wasn't sitting well with Jojo. It was something about the whole situation that *just-wasn't-sitting-well.*

Screw it, she went back to work. She hadn't been at her desk for five minutes.

"Hey, Josilyn... what you doing? Things working out?"

It was Wes.

"Hey, wassup...," Jocelyn told him. "Yeah, things are going good. What are you up to?" she asked now pretending as if she hadn't just seen him and Paula only 15 minutes earlier.

Wes asked her if she had gotten the hang of things and if she had needed any help with anything.

"Naw, I'm good. You did a good job at training me. Hell, I might even get as good as you are in a month or two," she joked.

"Yep... just might," Wes joked back but his smile didn't seem as genuine as he had hoped it to appear.

Jojo saw straight through it.

And why had he come sniffing around like he was trying to pick her or something? So what, if he was *banging the boss.* That was *his* business.

All Jojo wanted to do was to get her hours in, get her paychecks, and to get the hell out of there everyday... that's it.

No more, no less. *But here this nigga was acting all guilty and shit.*

Jojo's real side came out.

"Wes... what's up?" she asked raring back in her chair and looking him square in his eyes hombre a hombre style. Wes didn't expect such a masculine approach.

"What do you mean 'what's up' ?"

"I mean-- I'm busy trying to get these reports done so that I can get out of here like y'all. Man, it's Friday and out of all people *you* know how the boss is when she want what she wants."

Her last statement was like hitting a high note and struck a cord with Wesley. He flashed her another one of his fake smiles and took off.

"Something *is* going on," she concluded as she watched him strut away. "With his gay counterfeit looking ass," she added.

For some reason Jojo was pissed off now. And for some reason she now felt like going to get this shit straight about her check too.

Paula's office

"Yes, Josilyn... come on in," Paula told her.

Jojo stepped in. Things looked normal enough.

"Um--yes, Paula... I have a problem with my check," Jojo told her.

"Okay and what is the discrepancy?" Paula asked reaching out to accept the check being handed to her.

"Well--my hours. My pay is two days short," she said still noticing how cool and innocent Paula was acting.

Maybe she was better than Wes. She certainly was hiding it better.

Jojo moved in closer and pointed to a column on her paycheck stub that reflected her hours. Then she handed Paula a copy of her time clock hours that she had printed out from the system.

"Oh... I see," Paula said still not intimidated at the least and still in pro mode, "let's get a copy of this so that I can get payroll on it. We'll fix it, Jocelyn. Sorry."

Jojo figured that by moving in closer that she could've picked up on a vibe or something. Her senses were usually keen to these type of things especially when it came to another woman...considering. But nothing happened. Her meter still came up ice cubes. Paula showed no sign of guilt nor embarrass-ment.

After stepping over to the small copying machine that was tucked away in the corner Paula made a duplicate of Jojo's check and handed it back to her. Jojo accepted it and looked at it.

Paula apologized for the inconvenience, told her she'd handle it and basically dismissed her before walking back around to her desk and taking a seat. When she looked up Jojo was still standing there...still looking at her check.

Why?

Well, hell... Jojo didn't even know why. She was frozen.

"Yes, Josilyn... anything else?"

There was silence.

Paula had to mention Jojo's name again in order to get her attention.

"Jocelyn."

"Uh, yeah--sorry. I was just...um, just wanting to thank you for hiring me. You'll learn that I'm a *loyal* and very dedicated worker," she told her.

In other words..."I'm not going to snitch you and your 'BOY TOY' out. So, you ain't got to fire me."

That's what Jojo had wanted to say but she could only hope now that her true message wasn't lost in the translation.

"Well, thank you and you're quite welcomed," Paula answered still without fanfare. "Now if you'd excuse me, I really have to be getting these accounts ready for corporate."

And that was it.

Jojo left and Paula got back to work. By 3 o' clock the place was like a ghost town. Everyone had left...even Paula.

Don't want no man… Don't need no man…
Ain't got no man

Chapter Eleven

Jojo couldn't wait to get out to her car.
"Can you believe it?" she was yelling into her cell phone, "the woman had a foot long worth of tongue down that nigga throat! Yeah--all at work and *thangs!*"

Jojo was no longer in work mode she had flipped back to her normal element. She was sharing her day's events with Precious as she drove.

Precious listened, and then…

"Guess what?" she asked Jojo.

"What's that, sweetie?"

"All of the kids are gone," she said, "even my little man Shemar."

"Oh yeah?"

Jojo was excited. But that meant that her plans about doing something for all of them would now have to be changed.

"So what about the plans I had to do something nice for all y'all?" she asked.

Precious didn't want to ruin Jojo's mood so she just told her that it'll be best that they be alone 'tonight' and Jojo ran with that.

"Okay, Ma… give me time to cash my check, go home, show-er and shave and I'll be there. Okay?

"I'll see you then," Precious told her and the conversation ended.

On the other side of town

Paula was rushing home to shower and shave also. She hummed as she listened to the sounds of FLOETRY blaring through her speakers— "*All you gotta do is say yes... don't deny what you feel...*"

She loved that song and now as she drove home she realized that all of her butterflies were still there. They hadn't left. Not after the first, second, or the third time.

"But all you gotta do is just keep saying yes," she told herself.

She kept humming until she had *hummed* all the way home. Ironically the woman from the store crossed her mind... the one with the batteries.

"Yeah, well. I'd prefer butterflies over batteries any day," she told herself with a chuckle as she pulled her car into the garage.

She had made it home and had almost four hours to go until the time that she and Wes had agreed that they would meet. He was coming over to her place again.

Wes had told her that he had to get home and spend a little with Tinker and to get her settled with her babysitter   before he could shower or shave or get all fine for her.

Paula couldn't wait. And though she had told him to take his time, the truth was…she had went from no man to a fine man. From being alone and horny to getting it on the regular now. She had done this without even com-promising her career, her job, or her drive. She had it all for right now. Paula couldn't have been any more happier.

She had done what all she had to do and now there was only an hour left to go.

First would come conversation on the sofa. Maybe a kiss and then the dinner that she had prepared. A kiss again as she opened a bottle of wine.

More conversation across the table.

He'd flirt.

They'd pretend that they'd just met and that that first, second, or third time had never happened.

He'd pretend that he had to go.

"So Soon?" she'd ask him. "Please stay… maybe one more glass of wine."

And he'd agree…but they both were grown and they both knew about *buzzed driving.* He'd have to stay the whole night and they'd make love and he'd climb on top of her and she would him.

They'd exchange *oooh's* and swap out *ahhh's* all night long and she would take him inside of her and give herself to him again-- and again-- and again-- and again until he was spent and she was satisfied.

She'd wake up in the morning after wishing the moon a goodnight and once again she'd welcome her lover inside of her…and he'd oblige her.

He'd start her day off right and unlike that silly ass clock he would like down at her and wish her a good morning and she'd make sure that he screamed those three words of endearment that she had been waiting so long to hear. These are the words that started with the word I but didn't include the words love or you.

She wanted him to rattle from his toes up when he exploded inside of her.

Damn.

And Jojo made it to Precious.

Together they went out to get something to eat. They talked, laughed, ate and started drinking.

Jojo told Precious how she had walked up on her boss lady and the *scrub* that had trained her and how they were kissing their asses off.

Precious felt guilty… she wanted to say something and had tried but as soon as she had opened her mouth Jojo kissed her.

Precious wasn't supposed to let it get this far. What happened to the talk that she was supposed to have with Jojo? What happened to saying 'no'?

More drinks came as well as more advances from Jojo.

But these weren't advances were they? Advances were one-sided. Right?

And Precious had accepted everything that came her way. Right?

So that meant that they were on a two-way street. Of course they were.

"Come on…let's go back to your place," Jojo told her.

Chills ran down Precious' spine and her arm as she begin cursing herself for not being able to say no again. Before long they were back at her place and back in her bedroom--again.

The room wasn't spinning but her head was.

But Precious wasn't drunk with alcohol. She was drunk with emotions, so she didn't know what to say or to do.

Just as Jojo had laid her down and began undressing her she finally spoke.

"Wait," Precious tried but Jojo's passion burned.

She couldn't stop. She kissed more, fumbled more, unsnapped this and unbuttoned that not hearing a word of what Precious was saying.

"Wait! I said!"

And time stood still.

Jojo was on top of her. Drunk. Intoxicated. Feeling herself.

"What's wrong, baby?" she asked.

"Everything," Precious answered, "just everything. This ain't right."

Jojo just stared at her.

"Ain't right? What's not right about it?"

"That's what I've been trying to tell you since earlier," Precious admitted. "And that's why I told you that we needed to be alone… because I needed to talk to you."

"About what?" Jojo asked now raising herself from on top of Precious.

"About this. About what we're doing… *I'm* doing. This ain't me, Jojo. I mean-- you're cool and everything… and trust me, I *really* do appreciate all that you've done. But I can't do this no more so if I have to I'll pay you back for all the money you've spent on me or my kids I will. But I can't go on pretending anymore."

Precious paused and then hit her friend with the knock out punch.

"Jojo... it's over."

At that she crawled out of bed and walked over to her dresser and reached into her purse.

Jojo watched her still not saying anything. When Precious came back over and sat on the side of the bed she handed Jojo forty dollars.

"Here," she told her, "this is all the cash that I have on me right now but if you feel that I owe you more..."

Jojo cut her off.

"Keep the money," she told. "I'm not tripping about no money. I'm tripping about you."

"Me?" Precious asked still half undressed.

"Yeah... you," Jojo answered.

Was Jojo mad?

What did she mean about tripping off of Precious?

"I'm tripping on the fact that you're so concerned about what other people will say that you're actually cool with denying yourself of your own happiness. You *feel* good but you don't think it's good. You *say*

76

it's wrong but you feel so right. And then…
you say wait, stop, or no when everything
else--your eyes, body and heart says
'yes,take me and give me ecstasy'."

Time began to tick again… slowly.

"That's not how I feel, Jojo."
"Yes you do, sweetie."
"No it's not."
Jojo kissed her.
"Yes it is," she added.
Jojo tried to kiss her again.
"Jojo…please don't."
"Don't what?"
Kiss
"Don't…"
Kiss…Kiss.
"Don't do this, Jo-."
Jojo's kiss landed full on this time
"But I want you, baby," she told Precious,
"and I need you."
"You do?" Precious asked.
"Um-hmm…"
Kiss…kiss…long kiss.
"But what about… *mmm.* Damn Jojo,
baby."
"Come here," Jojo told her pulling her back
into the bed.

Precious gave in and laid beside her.

"Precious," Jojo said calling her lover's
name out softly.

"Yes," she answered weakly.

"Can I have you?" She asked now undressing Precious the rest of the way.

Precious closed her eyes.

"Shit, Jojo...I guess you already do."

Don't want no man... Don't need no man...
Ain't got no man

Chapter Twelve

Everyone seemed to be walking on clouds as the following week seemed to float by until around Wednesday. That's when things started changing.

Wes stopped accepting overtime *and* phone calls from Paula. This was a surprise to Paula considering that their last date was filled with good conversation, wonderful laughter, and great sex. Together they had taken passion to newer heights. He satisfied her and she him. Exhausted by morning they had challenged the night and won.

But Jojo's week hadn't been a problem except for a few surprise pop-ups from the lady that she felt had snuck up behind her that one time (*the chick with the attitude*).
She hadn't seen her having lunch with Paula anymore but ol' girl did seem to find herself in Jojo's face a couple of times or so. Each time she did she'd somehow always manage to relay a vibe of abhorrence that could've shook the average. But Jojo wasn't the average. Jojo would simply stand her ground, ignore the pink elephant and go on

about her day. She hadn't figured it out yet but this woman seemed to always act as if Jojo was in *her* way.

Wes kept his phone on vibrate as the calls kept coming... but he always kept ignoring them and he always sent them to voice-mail.
Paula was furious... worried... confused... and then furious all over again, especially when she saw him in the break room and he wouldn't speak.
"What the hell is going on?" she wondered.
She tried her best at staying focused but couldn't. Wes wasn't answering or returning her calls so something definitely was wrong... but what? For the life of her she couldn't figure it out.
She'd go home early.
At home she tried to read... *couldn't*. She tried watching a movie... *couldn't do that either.* Finally sleep became her only escape.

Don't want no man… Don't need no man…
Ain't got no man

Chapter Thirteen

Casual Night Out

"So you're just gonna keep hiding me from the kids?" Jojo was asking.

"Jojo don't," Precious begged, "you know I'm not ready to go there with that yet."

"Okay… I'm tripping. My bad," Jojo said apologetically and letting it go for now.

They were eating pizza… Precious' treat as the conversation took place.

It was a Wednesday night and the little pizzeria that they were at was crowded with people.

Jojo had finally figured out that Precious wasn't comfortable with PDA's so she chilled out with all the kissing and stuff while occassionally still shooting her her signature flirty re-marks across the table every now and again. Precious played cool with that and let her get away with a few.

The beginning of the week had signified to Jojo that she was going to be going through one of those type of cycles that women go through every month and by the look of what she was wearing--that phase had already begun. She damn near *really* looked like a man tonight. There was no makeup on... sweats... a hoodie pulled down low over her head...and cramps.

   Still sitting in their booth someone familiar caught Jojo's eye.
   It was the bitch from the job. The one with the attitude pro-blem.
   "Precious," Jojo said in a hushed voice while pulling her hood down even lower, "that's the chick from work that I was telling you about. The one that keep popping up on me."
   Precious looked. The woman was taking a seat at a booth not too far from them.
   "You hiding from her or something?" Precious asked.
   It almost sounded like there was a hint of jealousy there in her voice so much so that it caused Jojo to do a double take her way... Jojo made a mental note of it but left it alone for a later conversation.
   "There you go tripping. I'm not hiding," she corrected her, "I'm just not in the mood to be seeing her. She's already all up in my business at work. The last thing I want is for her..."
   And she went silent.

Jojo's speech ended mid-sentence. Precious stared at her. The words had gotten stuck in her throat.

"What?" Precious asked, "Jojo, what's wrong?"

It was at that time that another figure had came into the pizzeria and stepped into view. A man. Precious noticed the intenseness in Jojo's stare and followed it to its victim.

"Who is that?" she asked now watching the man who was sliding into the same booth that Jojo's friend from work had sat in.

The man was now kissing the woman.

"*Gay ass Wesley,*" Jojo whispered not being able to take her eyes off the couple.

"Ain't that some shit," she added.

Precious was trying to put together the puzzle of what Jojo was thinking but couldn't. Too many pieces were missing... but not for Jojo.

She had a very quick mind and sharp perception and all the pieces were falling right into place--*fast.*

"That's the dude from work that trained me," she told Precious.

" Huh? I thought you said that he was supposed to be kicking it with your boss... that manager lady?"

"Hell, that's what I thought but it looks like there's some bullshit going on somewhere. Wait... I've got to get some pictures of this."

As soon as she said it she was already digging in and pulling her camera phone out of her pocket. Precious didn't know why or what was going on but she was beginning to feel a little uncomfortable and nervous.

"What if they see us?" she asked.

"Sshhh," Jojo sounded wanting to hush Precious down.

Precious' mind journeyed a bit further.

"Hey, I ain't *fitna* be doing no fighting and shit up in here."

"Girl, be quiet. Wes is a punk. He ain't about to fight nobody."

And that was it.

Jojo finished snapping as many shots as she could before grabbing Precious and sneaking out of the restaurant.

But now what do she do? Was it even her business? It was obvious that Wes was playing a game... but what was the game about? Should she just stay neutral and allow them *grown folk* to handle their own business or what?

Jojo didn't know what to do. She'd have to figure it out... play it by ear. She drove in silence and after dropping Precious off drove on to her own home to think and contemplate her next move. While thinking she wondered to herself... *"but who will I be helping... or hurting?"*

That night she tossed and turned until sun up.

Don't want no man... Don't need no man...
Ain't got no man

Chapter Fourteen

Thursday Morning... Jojo was still thinking what to do?

Punch-in at the time clock.
Go around the *long* way to my department.
Do my job.
And mind my own business.
Those were Josilyn Hatcher's plans. The plans that she had come up with after wrestling with her sheets the whole night through, til now.

She logged in at her terminal, began processing reports, and then she smelled him. Jojo knew that smell from anywhere. She had trained beside it for damn near a week or so and here it was somewhere close to her again.

She looked up just in time enough to see Wesley passing by dressed in a very nice business suit with what looked like an entourage of small-time Fortune 500 wannabes trailing behind him.

Paula sat in her office. Still mad. Still confused. Still professional and busy. Her phone rang. She could see that it was the line from upfront that the front office girl would use. Just as she had picked up the handset to answer her office door flew open... *rudely*.

"Hang up the phone, Ms. Martin," another black woman was saying. But without warning or waiting immediately stepped up and placed a finger on the button on Paula's phone and disconnected her.

Paula recognized the woman. Sharon Hornsby. She was *Paula's* boss.

If Paula was 'the boss lady' then this was 'the *Big* boss lady' Sharon Hornsby... Vice President... second only to Thomas Hornsby, her husband and the President and founder of the company.

Something was wrong and somebody was in trouble... *big* trouble

Paula looked and searched out the faces that were in her office staring back at her. She went from Mrs. Hornsby and others to a few men that she didn't know or recognize, and then to her HR Manager... and then to who? *Wesley?*

Her heart tightened in her chest.

"What is this about?" she asked firmly.

Paula's dignity was still intact.

The answer came from the VP as she slammed a small stack of papers upon Paula's desk.

"This--Ms. Martin is about a full investigation into a Sexual Harassment case that has came across not only my desk but my husband's desk as well...which is very embarrassing and has attacked the very foundation of what we've strived so long to bring strength and distinction to."

Paula's jaw dropped and though she knew that at a time like this, especially as things were happening as they were, to look at Wes right now would almost definitely be considered as an admission of guilt. But she couldn't help it. Reflexes won over brains. Her eyes beamed and shot daggers straight through him.

He didn't bulge.

One of the unknown guys, his leading lawyer presumably, stepped up and dropped an even heavier sounding stack of papers on her desk right in front of her.

"Your copy," he told her, "we'll also be filing another formal complaint with the criminal courts, *Ms. Martin.*"

The way that he said her name made it sound like shit. Paula was only hoping that at the moment...it tasted like shit as well.

Then as if on cue he turned around, entourage in tow and walked out of the office... his client following.

"Ms. Taylor," the VP was now saying to her HR Manager, "please retrieve all of our office keys and security cards from Ms. Martin and relieve her of her duties--until further notice."

Paula was still in mid-bewilderment. She couldn't believe it. Things were happening way too fast.

She also realized that she had been sitting down the whole time as she felt herself now beginning to stand though still in shock.

Mrs. Hornsby stepped forward once more and now almost nose to nose with Paula spoke softly through her teeth.

Paula could see that she was pissed.

"Your actions has brought disgrace to my company and to the dignity of all the women whom I've placed in leadership positions, Ms. Martin."

Mrs. Hornsby paused for affect and then hit her with the whammy when she added, "I hope you're proud of yourself, *Sistah*,"... and left.

Paula stood there speechless. She could barely hear the words being spoken to her.

"Ms. Martin," the HR lady was saying, "your things, please."

Don't want no man... Don't need no man...
Ain't got no man

The Epilogue

Jojo had snuck back around the long way to see 'what the hell' was going on in the boss lady's office. What she saw short-stopped her in her tracks. She hadn't even made it to the end of the row of cubicles when she saw *ol' girl*, yeah--the one with the attitude, peeping around the corner.

She even took a picture of that.

"What the hell are *you* doing?" Jojo asked this time scaring the shit out *her*.

"What the fu--," the woman almost screamed damn near jumping out of her skin.

"You sure have been sneaking around a lot, lady," Jojo told her.

The lady regained her composure and counter-attacked Jojo with a statement of her own.

"You'd better stay in your lane, lesbo... or you can get marched up out of here too."

With that said she took a step forward to leave but Jojo stepped in front of her.

"Look--I don't know what you've got against Paula or what the fuck y'all trying to do but I bet she'll be *real* interested in these pictures that I've got of you and Wes from the pizza place last night."

The bitch with the attitude face went blank and lifeless but Jojo didn't wait for the rest of the results. She stepped around her and headed straight for Paula's office.

The HR lady had left Paula alone to clear out her desk and her office.

"Paula...," Jojo said stepping in and startling her *ex*-boss.

Paula looked up...

"Josilyn, now is not a good time. I'm sorry but anything company related should be discussed with your supervisor, Jayla. Okay?"

Jojo didn't see any tears but she knew women enough to know that something was wrong. She heard it in Paula's voice.

"What's going on? What are you doing, Boss Lady...are you leaving?"

"I'm fired," Paula admitted still not looking up, "and I am no longer your *boss* lady," she added. The latter part of what she said came with a forced chuckle and smile.

Jojo didn't know what to say...

"Boss Lady," she said again this time causing Paula to finally look at her, "I came by your office last Friday because of something other than my check. I came because I was mad and I thought that you were playing games with me. Well... not just you but you and Wes."

Paula's heart skipped...

"Me and Wes?" she asked.

"Yeah... I saw y'all kissing here in your office last week and thought that y'all had seen me too and was trying to pick me but I realized that you wasn't. I also realized something else other than that...your friend that you're always having lunch with?"

"What friend?" Paula asked searching her mind.

"That nosey one with the attitude. The bitch you be with in the break room all the time," Jojo said with anger.

"Tameeka?" Paula answered not too sure.

It was the office mate that she'd known for years and it was the only one whom she'd ever ate with in the break room.

"Yeah! Her! They set you up, Boss Lady! There's no doubt in my mind that they did. Now--I understand that I might be a little soulful and ghetto...maybe even rough around the edges when it comes to this corporate stuff. But one thang I know is that I ain't stupid, Boss Lady... and game recognizes game. That dude Wesley and that bitch that's supposed to be your so-called friend Tameeka... them motherfuckas got you fired. And if you ask me...they *fucking* too!"

Jojo explained everything to Paula... "Here--take my phone it's pre-pay," she told her. "I'll get my number cut off and transferred to another phone later but look at these pictures... they'll express a thousand words. And maybe your lawyer can use them."

The HR lady appeared back in the doorway.

"Excuse me," Jojo said stepping around her and leaving her *ex*-Boss Lady's office.

Paula stared down at the small phone that Josilyn had left behind. It was at that moment that she remembered the speech that Josilyn had given her only days earlier when she had appeared in her office... something about being *loyal and dedicated.* ..characteristics that neither Wesley nor Tameeka possessed. She finished her packing and left.

On her way out she realized how light she felt.

No reports... no computer bag... no more deadlines... and not a clue as to what her future would bring.

She saw the pictures... and recognized the people. Saw the plan and saw how it was all so clear now.

Never had she actually laid eyes on the mysterious '*Tinker*' nor had she ever actually heard her voice or spoke to her.

And what about Jayla, Wesley's supervisor? Was she somehow wrapped up in all this mess?

Remembering back, *she* had been the one to actually hire Wesley.

She called her. Jayla had heard what happened.

"I had nothing to do with it," she sincerely pleaded to Paula while adding "Tameeka was the one who brought him to *my* attention. I went off of her story."

Paula believed her. She'd get to the bottom of this and she'd make sure that the people responsible would pay.

She'd go to her lawyer tomorrow morning and together they'd sit down, download pictures, get verbal statements and affidavits and everything else they needed... and they'd win--not only for her but for the many other women or men who had fallen victim to lies and scandal like this

Yep, that was her plan for tomorrow.

But for now... she was tired. She was scared and she was alone.

As she pulled her BMW into her garage the cd that had been playing since she'd left the office slowly ended one significant song and rolled into the next.

Paula pushed the remote button to allow the garage door to lower itself back down.

She sat there in the car, in the dark, and in her world of loneliness.

Marsha Ambrosia's doubled-edged sword mocked her with the same lyrics that only days earlier had been a comfort to her soul.

*There is only one for me...*she tuned

Marsha sang and Paula sung along with her. At first with a smile because she was free. And then with a tear which she wasn't quite sure about.

She wiped the first... and then the second... and the third one too. The fourth one she wanted to feel so she closed her eyes and allowed it to sting. She allowed it to remind her of that one last long night of passion that had ultimately cost her her job. It had not only cost her her career but everything else that she had worked hard for. It hurt.

It reminded her of Wes' tongue as she laid on her stomach and allowed him to use it on her as he left a trail of moisture and fire from the sensitive part at the back of her neck all the way down to the small of her back.

She had moaned. She had turned over and kissed him. She had allowed him to enter her… and she liked it.

But it was over now. No more lies. No more deception. No longer would she torture herself because of her mistake.

Paula had did all that she could and became all that she had wanted.

She had worked her way up the side of the mountain. Ironically it had been that same moutian that she had just been thrown off of. She couldn't believe how life had played such a terrible trick on her. It was cruel.

But hey… no longer would she cry and never again would she have to hurt. She had made up her mind.

She was tired. She'd sing herself to sleep.

As she sung--her eyelids began getting heavier as she felt herself growing even more sleepier.

She looked up.

When she did she began wishing the moon a goodnight while laying her head back and deciding to sing one last song.

"God help me," she mumbled… *"God help us all"*.

Paula Martin was officially pronounced dead by a Coroner

Cause of death… asphyxiation (A lack of oxygen or excess of carbon monoxide in the body that results in unconsciousness and often death).

She never turned her car's engine off once she pulled into her garage.

But the question I ask…was it an accident or was it an escape?

You tell me

The End

The Left Hand... Third Finger

#

By A.e. Santi

You are now entering into a separate story.
Book Two

The Left hand...Third Finger

*Mar'riage (mar'ij) n. 1. Legal union of a
man and woman
2. a wedding. –mar'riage-a-able, adj.*

Chapter One

Courtney Peterson and Belinda Freeman
began as high school sweethearts over
twenty something years ago. But now they
were the Peterson *family*, together sharing
more than just a formal last name.

Along with the last name also came the
sharing of a mortgage, some utility bills,
medical responsibilities, car notes, and a
son...Josh.

Josh was a good kid...a smart kid. He
didn't do drugs, was very mannered and
respectable... and he loved his mom.

She along with the help of his dad had
raised him well. But having finally made it
through high school Josh without much
thought decided to skip college altogether.
He wanted to join the ever increasing work
force related world of grease monkeys.

He wanted to become a mechanic and as
time went by he eventually wanted to begin
buying, rebuilding and reselling cars *"like
on Gas Monkey,"* he would declare.

He argued with his parents about it saying that while doing so he'd also play his part in helping to keep the city clean and free of the many eyesores that were left behind along the side of the streets by people who didn't even care about how the city looked.

Courtney and Belinda understood him but they wanted their boy in college. *Real* college. Especially considering that he was smart enough to go almost any one that he wanted to go to. But that's not what he wanted to do.

"Well…are you at least going to go to one of those trade schools that they got going on these days?" Belinda had asked hoping that her husband would come up with a better argument than she could at the time.

Her eyes dotted between Courtney and Josh.

"Hell-- say something," she thought.

But Courtney just stared at his son…which didn't bother Josh because he had already made up in his mind that he wasn't going anywhere and he wasn't leaving his mother.

"Why not A.T.I.?" Courtney had finally asked.

"Yeah Josh, why not…?" She stopped and looked at her husband hoping that he'd finish the question.

"A-T-I," her husband concluded for her.

Belinda Knew that there were schools out there that were available for that kind of vocational training but the names of those institutions had failed her at the time

"Dad, *Another Trained Idiot?*" Josh Joked...

And they all laughed.

"Yes, Josh," Courtney told him, "in spite of the acronyms."

The room went silent for a minute.

"Well at least promise us that you'll enroll and start after you get settled on a job and start making a little money," Belinda added as the Peterson's family discussion began winding to a close.

Josh thought about it. His plans were to just go straight into a shop and to start building from there, but winning half a battle with his parents was better than not winning at all so he gave in.

"Promise?" she asked.

"I promise, Mom."

And that was it.

Josh honestly didn't have any idea how things were going to fan out by the end of the discussion but ultimately he had come out a winner... which was much to his surprise.

But he had to win he told himself. This time *this* discussion was more than about just a failing grade… or a car for his senior year… or even a tattoo before the age of 18 (which his father had argued that he'd have to wait until the age of 21 instead because basing the fact that in order to stand the pain Josh would more than likely have to be drunk when he got the damn thing forcing him to wait until he could legally buy his own liquor).

"Yes," Josh told himself, "this time was about not staying too far from home and being afraid to leave his mother alone with his dad, keeping his anger at bay, or respecting the man that he had grown to hate so much. It was about so much more."

Years ago, as Josh grew up, he had many times laid awake in his bed during those late night occasions when his dad, finally exhausted from chasing the many different night demons that he loved so much would drunkardly come home only to argue and fight with his wife, Josh's mom.

He would just lay in his bed, cry and listen.

These arguments often times turned into screaming matches which eventually became just flat out physical and violent. As a kid Josh heard it all and it bothered him.

It bothered his grades, his attitude and it bothered his regards toward what marriage meant or even supposed to have meant. But he had never let his mom nor his dad in on his pain… nor his secret.

He had a plan…a plan to one day marry a beautiful woman, treat her good and in the fashion that man had stood and promised before the heavens that he'd treat her, cherish her, and provide for her. They would live happily ever after…or at least until death did do them part and he'd never hit her like his dad would his mom.

Nor would he ever cheat on her. This is something that his dad did too. In fact, in Josh's mind his dad did all the things to his mom that a husband was never supposed to do…and he hated it.

It was months later almost a year even before Josh had actually enrolled into a technical school that promised him the formal and credited education of being a certified and advanced mechanic. Atleast one that would receive higher pay. And although this was a somewhat dirty and grimey profession that had been chosen the money had finally begun looking a lot better.

"Josh!" he heard his boss yell out.

"Yeah! What's up?"

"Got an oil change for ya! Silver Gallant!"

In no time Josh was off of the stool that he'd sit at during the times there wasn't anything to get done.

His boss didn't mind.

He'd be on his phone either texting, checking his email, posting on *facebook*...something.

Even when at home Josh could always be found doing something with his phone or computer.

Three things he loved...electronics, cars, and money.

Ron, the shop's owner, handed him a set of keys as he passed.

Josh hadn't made it to the service office in order to pick up the keys or the vehicle's work order because Ron was more than happy to bring the items to him especially considering that Ron had just recently began a workout and dieting regiment that he swore would have him right for the upcoming summer months.

In hopes of losing weight and burning calories he had been ripping and running around the shop all week trying to pitch in or go that extra mile...literally.

"How many pounds have you already lost so far, Ron C"? Josh asked spinning on his heels to head outside where he'd find the awaiting Mitsubishi.

"Man, I don't know. Two…three, maybe," he heard Ron saying as his voice faded off behind the glass door that was swinging close after he had exited it.

Josh was kinda laughing to himself as he approached the driver's side door of the car that he'd be working on.

The humor was that he already knew what Ron was still saying when he was walking out which was the same thing that he told everyone that inquired about his day-to-day weight loss.

He'd always say, "Man… I told you that I'm doing this thing collectively…so stop asking me every day about how much weight I've lost.'

So now--everybody asked him just to piss him off…*everyday*.

The door of the Mitsubishi swung open.

"Oh--hi," a cute young woman said, "I was just getting my earbuds. Let me get out of your way."

"No, you're cool," Josh told her trying to hold his composure.

She hadn't scared him but she had shocked him. She was gorgeous.

"Take your time," he added.

"Just let me find my…," she said flipping open a center console and rambling through it. Finally she came out with a hot pink set of dangling wires. "Here they are," she added holding them up as she slid around Josh with a smile.

Now as he sat in the driver's seat of the girl's car staring through its windshield at her butt he was frozen and keeping his eyes glued to the seat of her jeans watching her as she walked away.

The girl was fine. *Real* fine. And being fine was a good thing not to mention that right now the girl was definitely registering as a double threat in Josh's book.

She had booty and beauty.

"Damn," he said starting her car and pulling it into one of the shop's service bays that they used to change oil.

He did the job in its usual amount of time but thought about the car's owner every minute as he did. He couldn't get her off his mind…this is the kind of girl that he had been waiting on for a long *long* time.

He had plans for her.

Josh stuck around the office a little longer than normal. He would usually pull the serviced on vehicle back around to the front of the shop, drop off its keys and sign off on the work order. If another job wasn't waiting he'd always head back to his stool and begin attacking his *facebook* account all over again.

But not this time. This time he clumsily fumbled around the office--umm...*ear hustling*. Yeah. That's what he was doing. He was ear hustling...trying to hear or catch on to something that wasn't any of his business.

Luckily he hadn't been given a work order to sign off on.

Earlier Ron had only given Josh keys...no work order.

Work orders included and documented names which before now never seemed important to Josh. An oil change was an oil change...a tune up, a tune up... and an inspection was just another dog-gone inspection. But now for some strange and somewhat intriguing reason Josh wanted to attach a name. As-sociate it with a face and a booty.

He had been waiting on that damn work order.

And now after trying so hard not to look like a damn fool after almost 10 minutes of mixing stuff together...first the coffee, then a little creamer, then a little sugar, then a little more creamer, a touch more of coffee, some sugar...stir. Sip...blow...sip...more sugar, more ear hustling, more looking crazy, and then finally he heard it.

"September, that'll be…"

Ron had barely gotten that part out before, like *poof*…Josh appeared right there beside him and somewhat crowding his space.

Ron stopped and looked up at Josh.

"Yeah, what's up?" he asked.

"Nuttin'," Josh answered looking crazy. And then, "…and what's up with the coffee, bro? You don't drink coffee."

Josh handed it over.

"Yeah I know. It's for you."

"But I don't drink coffee neither," Ron said.

It was an awkward moment. One like when complete silence consumes a room where all is still and no one knows quite what to do…or to say.

"Well, I just *um*-made it just in case you-- well…in case you *might* need it."

"*Might* need it ?" Ron asked.

Damn that sounded stupid. He looked at September. She had that '*yeah it did sound stupid*' look on her face but still smiled because even though he was acting goofey, he was kind of cute still.

OG, supposed to be Triple *OG* Ron just kept looking upside the boy's head tripping because he had never seen Josh acting so girl struck. It was funny to him. But he knew the business. Hell, he was supposed to be the *old school player*. Atleast that's what he told them.

"Okay…well, thank you young brother. But can I also get a little elbow room to go with this *whatever it is* that I might be needing?"

"Oh yeah…right," Josh said backing away while once again glancing across the counter at this girl who was somehow sweeping him off his feet.

Ron was finally able to get back to his job explaining to the customer the terms of her warranty. He explained her charges and what was used and he also included an open invitation to bring her vehicle back for any further servicing. September made small talk as she thanked him and surrendered her debit card.

As the man in front of her swiped it and waited she found herself searching and eyeing the area in hopes of seeing that little cute greasy guy again. He was gone.

"Was that the guy that changed my oil?" she asked Ron.

"Yep," he answered, "I don't know where he went."

The lady got her receipt and headed out the door.

Just making it to her car and as she began reaching for the door

"Let me get that for you, "she heard someone say.

And he ended it with, "September."

"Oh, so you know my name now?" she answered.

"Yep. Paid my dues of looking like a damn fool just to get it."

They both laughed which was a good thing because that was a sign that Josh was racking up points

"I'm Josh," he said introducing himself. He waited for her to shake his hand which was now extended out but instead she looked at it and gave a little sexy frown.

"Oh-- my bad."

Josh realized that after finishing up with her car he was in such a rush to get back to the service counter to see her and catch her name that it had completely slipped his mind to *Gook* and wash up.

They air dapped … you know, dapped without touching.

He opened her car door for her and after she got in used a shop towel to wipe the handle back off when he closed it.

Her window slid down.

"Thanks," she told him.

There weren't any other cars coming in so Josh took advantage of this opportunity to put his macking down.

The conversation took form as they began discussing if they had any other significant people in their lives.

"*No.*"

Kids?

"*Oh, hell no. Not until marriage.*"

School?

"*Yes.*"

Josh had graduated earlier that year from his trade school but she was still going. She only had a little ways to go to finish. They seemed compatible.

Compatibility brought about exchange...the exchange of smiles, phone numbers, and promises to call... *after her last class tonight.*

September left Josh standing in her review mirror. He watched her car as it pulled all the way out the shop's parking lot.

Satisfied he headed back inside.

"You wanna empty out this poison, youngsta?" Ron said as soon as he hit the door."I already don't drink coffee as it is but this--I sho nuff had to spit this mess out."

Ron had joked and chided Josh for the remainder of the day and night until they had closed shop…and although Josh *knew* how stupid he must have acted and appeared earlier the end justified the means. He had somehow impressed September enough that, regardless, she still liked him enough to give up all those smiles and those most precious and coveted digits. Her phone number.

He couldn't wait to get home nor for her to finally get out of her last class. He'd wait for her call and he'd step up his game… *and* his swagger.

Josh wasn't about to drop the ball with this one. She was what he'd been looking for and waiting on for a long time now.

"If only she knew," he said talking to himself, "*if only she knew.*"

THE LEFTHAND... THIRD FINGER

En-gage'ment n. 1. The act of engaging or
the state of being engaged
2. an appointment
3. an agreement to marry
4. a battle

Chapter Two

Months later they found themselves in
love and almost about to get married.
Damn.
How did all that happen?
So fast?
It was a whirlwind love and their
relationship had moved in warp speed.
But now Josh was more furious than
embarrassed. Or was that he more ashamed
than upset?

"But how in the hell could he just *not*
show up, Mom?"
Josh was saying this to Belinda as he
added, "And he's still not here!"
Together, he and Belinda were washing,
drying, and putting away dishes. Dishes

which were her best china, brought out and used for special occasions only--tonight being one of them.

But where was Courtney?

It began again months...almost a year ago. It was shortly after Josh's graduation from *ATI*... or maybe even before.
But who knows?
Courtney had started up again. The drinking, the late nights, the scream matches, and though Josh couldn't be sure yet possi-bly the violence with his mom too.
He couldn't believe it. After doing so well.
DAMN!!!
But why? Why ruin it all again? Why break down again what so carefully had been built back up?

That night after finally retiring to his room and getting alone to himself it infuriated Josh enough to tears.
He had tried to forgive his father and had even come close.
There had been a few special times where he and his dad would somehow find themselves in one or two of those supposed to be father-son moments when knowledge, heritage and the characteristics of a man were supposedly handed down.

"Marriage is sacred," his *sober* father had told him one time."It makes a man complete. He comes full circle. Like this ring," he added holding up his left hand and using his thumb to rub along the smoothness of the golden piece of precious metal encircled around his third finger.

"So what would you say if I told you that I wanted to get married?"

Josh's father answered him that day with a statement that was just as simple as the chuckle that came with it.

"First you've got to get engaged, son."

And now here it was on the night of a planned formal dinner with his parents where he had set his sights on proposing to his girl, September... Dad was nowhere to be found.

Tears stung the sides of Josh's face as he lay upon his bed re-igniting the hate that he had inside of him and redefining his plan.

"He'd get his...no matter what or how long it took," he vowed that night.

There was a knock at his bedroom door.

Belinda could see sudden darkness around the frame and the bottom of her son's door as she stood waiting for his okay for her to come in. She had learned years ago that though her only child was very much masculine like his father, his emotional characteristics had solely came from her.

Lights out meant that he was crying and preferred that no one saw it or knew it. She opened the door slightly.

"Can I come in?" his mother asked him rhetorically and though she was basically already entering she dared not turn any lights on.

"Yeah, sure."

Belinda walked over to his bed…"men cry in the dark," she said sitting beside her baby. But her baby didn't look at her and there weren't any words for her either.

With only the light from the hallway stealing its way into Josh's room and betraying the darkness that he had preferred to be blanketed by it was easy for Belinda to confirm that, yes indeed, her baby had been crying. His eyes glimmered still moist from his tears.

"Are you okay?" she asked.

"I am now," Josh told her.

"I agree. He should've been here. Tonight was special to you *and* her," Belinda added as a second thought.

"So… did I do the right thing?" Josh asked seeking approval and acceptance form his mom.

"Depends?"

"Depends on what?" he asked finally looking up at her.

"Do you really love her? And do you *really* think that you're ready for marriage?"

"I proposed to her tonight, didn't I? So I guess that's a yes and *another* yes."

Belinda just looked on casually allowing her son to vent if he wanted to. She was doing her best at trying to be mother *and* father tonight.

"Well--I enjoyed myself tonight seeing it all unfold," she admitted knowing that she was still on the losing end of the no-win battle she had entered in on.

She, too, was disappointed at her husband's absence on the night that their only child had asked the woman that he loved to marry him. Sadness filled her as she stepped out of Josh's room pulling the door to behind her.

That night a terrible dream came upon Josh.

He had heard somewhere along the way that man should never allow his anger to fall upon his pillow... meaning, never go to sleep ticked off. But on this night he did.

At some point during the night Josh's vision came bearing a very un-easing message.

In his dream he and his father were together working on an old school car of some sort. They had been deep in its engine. "Go start it up," Courtney had told him. At about that time Courtney's cell phone had also rung. By the way that he had all of a sudden smiled and lowered his voice Josh could tell that more than likely it was one of his few or many women that he would sneak out on his mother with.

But…Josh had done what he was told. He turned the key to the ignition.

At that instant a most piercing scream struck through the air. A scream deeply laden with pain and more pain. Josh bolted from the driver's seat and ran to the front of the car. Looking down he saw his father on the ground clutching and squeezing his left hand as blood flowed through his fingers.

Tears were streaming down both eyes. And though Josh could've reached out instantly to help his injured father, he didn't. He could only stand there and watch as Courtney screamed and used every four letter curse word available.

"Help me up!" his dad demanded.

Josh did as told but what shocked him was when his father was reaching out to grab at his hand he could see that somehow, through his misdirected focus, possibly due to his talking on the phone to his mistresses, his hand must have gotten caught up in the pathway of the engine's old fashioned metal radiator fan.

Courtney held his left hand out. Josh saw that his third finger was missing. It had been cut off and his wedding band flung across the yard.

"You cheating bastard!" he heard a woman screaming, "get the hell away from me!"

Josh struggled to find her. He struggled so much so that he began waking up...but only to discover that the woman's voice he heard was not part of some crazy sick dream, it was his mother's voice and he was *not* dreaming.

Courtney had made it home late-- again. And he and Belinda were at each other's throats--again. But it seemed that she had a bigger chunk of flesh than he this time, until...

***Whoppp*!**

It was the sound of flesh against flesh... a frightening sound that instantly caused Josh to jump out of his bed and begin rushing to his mom's rescue.

"Don't hit her no more!" Courtney heard from behind him.

Belinda, still holding her face, saw her son standing in her and her husband's bedroom door with a butcher's knife in his hand.

"Oh my God," she said nervously as she and Courtney looked on.

"Don't ever hit my mother again!" Josh snapped.

But this time he said it with a definitive meaning of intent.

"You pulling a knife on me, boy?" Courtney questioned.

Courtney's words were slightly slurred, evidence of his alcohol induced absence from the family dinner.

"Just don't hit her again, Dad--or I'll…"

"You'll what!" Courtney yelled taking a step toward Josh.

Josh raised the knife and tightened his grip.

"No!" Belinda screamed. "No, Courtney! No Josh!"

She couldn't believe it. How could it have come to this?

This family? My husband? My son?

She quickly ran over to stand between the two.

"I SAID NO!" she yelled once again but this time as she stood in the middle with both of her arms extended in both directions.

"So you think it's two men of the house now, boy?" Courtney angrily asked Josh.

"Naw...can't be. I became the only man in this house the day you started putting your hands on my mama."

Silence filled the air. Tears filled eyes. And sorrow entered hearts. Tonight would definitely be a night to remember...for everyone.

Josh was alone in his room again but this time he was refusing to cry. His anger wouldn't let him. There was no way that he'd ever change his mind again. That's it. He made his final decision.

Tomorrow he'd talk with September and together they'd start early with his plan. She'd understand. She'd have to.

He had planned this thing and had been placing every single piece of the puzzle strategically in its own special little slot.

Strangely a smile now began to crowd his face.

No longer was he sad... nor angry... neither mad nor upset. He was confident now in his faith of knowing that surely things were going to be alright and that he was going to live happily ever after, even if it took doing it without his father.

Plan -ing 1. to make a plan of (a structure, etc)
2. to devise a scheme for doing, etc.
3. to have in mind as a project or purpose.
Vi. to make plans.

Chapter Three

It was like a puzzle and everything had to be fitted into its place just right.
The dinners, the moments alone, the meetings, the wedding...everything.
Even *after* the wedding these moments and days would become even more of an importance than before. Timing was everything.
Josh couldn't believe just how understanding and willing September had been. It didn't take much nor long to convince her. He felt that somehow them meeting one another was a part of their perfect fate. They connected and discovered love and had somehow even forged a trust together.

The months rolled by and as the wedding drew closer Josh's anger eventually subsided somehow. He had begun spending more time at home while also inviting September to come join him. It was all for the sake of familyhood.

"It'll bring you and my parents closer together," he had also explained. And it did.

But it wasn't all *that* easy. There was still plenty tension in the air. A lot had went down and a lot had to be fixed.

Belinda, still the hopeful wife, had one night sat down to a long talk with Courtney begging for him not to mess up things between he and Josh again.

"Try for me," she had pleaded, "at least until after the wedding."

"Try how?" Courtney asked.

"Talk to him. Hell, apologize for goodness sake. And it wouldn't hurt to speak to his girlfriend every now and again. After all-- she is his fiancée and will be your daughter-in-law soon."

Courtney had been ashamed and embarrassed about what had happened that last time that he had came back home drunk from one of his affairs and night out. He hadn't planned on things getting out of hand as they had, especially not going as far as having his own son threaten him with a weapon the way that he did. He had only wanted to cause a little friction between himself and Belinda in order to create himself an out.

You know... pick a fight... make her mad enough to leave the room... rush...take a quick shower...and be in the clear for having to have sex that night
She'd be too pissed off.
But it didn't happen that way and neither did he know that he had somehow missed a very important dinner date.
Hopefully he'd be able to patch up things and make up for it.

Days later

"Are you up for having a barbecue this evening?" Belinda asked.
"Today? Kind of a last minute notice wouldn't you think?" her husband stated.
"Yeah, it is. But your son called and asked. He said that he and September both had took today off from their jobs. And that's what they wanted to do today. Have a barbeque. It's a start, Courtney."
"So I guess I'm the one doing the cooking...right?"
"Why not..." Belinda flirted, " you're the baddest man I know on the grill."
This welcomed a shared moment of laughter together. They hugged and kissed.
Belinda was so happy and delighted about pulling her family back together again, not to mention the added member, that she

literally felt herself floating. Tonight would be special…and she was so ready for it.

The smell of smoked links, chicken, burger patties and steaks had no longer than 30 minutes or so began flooding and floating around the air when…

"*Whew*! That smells good," Courtney heard coming from behind him.

He had just finished moving some meat around on the grill. When he turned around there stood Belinda, Josh and September smiling at him. September had been the one who had spoken and made the comment.

"Hey, you two," he greeted but very shocked. Luckily he did a damn good job at hiding it because had he not hid his thoughts it would've been very disastrous..with a hell of a price to pay.

But no one noticed so it seemed or atleast he hoped, because alongside his wife and son all Courtney Peterson could see was September…which is one of the shortest months in the year wearing an even *shorter* pair of what young people today would call "*Coochie Cutters*."

"This wasn't going to be an easy day to get through," Courtney thought to himself.

Later on that night

"I really do like Josh's girlfriend, September. But at first she never really struck me as the kind of girl to dress like that. You see what she had on? How do *you* feel about what she was wearing with her butt hanging all out and stuff?" Belinda was rambling on and asking Courtney.

Men who've been married for a while know that this is a trick question. Women oftentimes be sneaky in their ways of investigating their husband's whereabouts, thoughts, and actions by shielding their true curiosities behind real simple questions.

"Shoot, baby...I really wasn't paying no attention. Hell, you know how these youngsters be dressing nowadays."

Good answer.

But he was lying. In fact, every chance the older Peterson man got he was stealing a glance at September *especially* if no one else was around. Surprisingly, there were even a few times when he'd actually thought that the girl was flaunting certain body parts on purpose...and flaunting them toward him

Courtney had shrugged it off and counted it as either coincidental or that maybe it was just his own lustful nature tripping.

"But one thing for sure," he thought…
"the girl *was* fine."

In an inwardly and secretly way he was proud of his son for even bagging such a nice catch.

"Just like his father," he said to himself that night knowing that Josh would've never agreed about that had he heard it.

If anything they were worlds apart. Even the thought of it would've driven Josh insane with anger. So…no, he was nothing like his father.

More months passed and with each Josh's plan became more and more alive. Everything was falling into place. Together they had spent more time with the parents…more time planning…and more time executing their plans.

Things were just right. Couldn't have been better...or could they have been.

One day

Courtney was at home relaxing in his recliner watching some sort of sports special when the house phone rang.

"Hello," he answered.

"Hi, Mr. Peterson. This' September. Did I catch you at a bad time?"

"Naw, baby…what's up?" he asked now sounding a little more perkier.

"I need your help," she said. "I went out and bought Josh a new computer desk for when he moves in but it's all unassembled and I want it to be a surprise."

Courtney was all ears.

"Could you come over and put it together for me? I mean, if it's not asking too much," she added.

"Um--no, it's not asking too much," he quickly answered.

In no time Courtney had received September's address to her apartment by text and was out the door.

He had remembered that September had said that she wanted it to be a *surprise* to Josh. She never said anything about it being one to Belinda…so why didn't Courtney call his wife to *atleast* let her know where he was going?

Maybe old habits die hard but this was supposed to be innocent and ofcourse this was nothing like sneaking off to be with one of his hidden women of the past. This was his soon to be daughter-in-law.

So, what was up with Courtney?

Was he feeling guilty about something or was it the fact that Courtney may have been harboring his own pitiful-*ass* intent-ions to begin with?

He drove with excitement as he felt for a CD case that normally sat in the passenger seat beside him. It wasn't there.

The previous day he and Belinda had rode together to the mall. They'd gone in order for Courtney to get fitted for his tuxedo for Josh's wedding. Belinda was in one of those ol' mushy type modes after that so after returning to the car she had dug out one of her favorites cd's from the case and tossed the rest into the back seat. He finally found it. Out came the Maxwell and in went the Jeezy. Courtney was tripping.

September was almost sure that she had heard some bass pulling up in the parking lot.

"*I know he ain't,*" she said to herself with a chuckle.

Seconds later her boyfriend's dad was knocking at her door.

"What's up?" he asked walking in.

When he passed September noticed an aroma that was too fresh of a smell for the semi-wrinkled look that Courtney was sporting.

"He must've sprayed something on in the car," she thought.

But Courtney still tried his best at acting normal even after seeing September fully dressed this time, which was quite a disappointment.

He had worked himself up in the car all the way over hoping for an attire that would again send his imaginative thoughts soaring.

They made small talk as September escorted her soon to be father-in-law into *her* and her soon to be *husband's* bedroom.

"There's the box…and I want it set up right over there in that corner," she pointed.

Courtney put down the small tool belt that he had brought in with him and after dragging the big box that contained the unassembled computer desk over to the corner which September had suggested, he opened it and began his project.

At first September stood by and watched. Then she sat on the edge of the bed still looking on.

"Want anything to drink?" she kindly suggested, "I could at least do that for you since you're the one using all them muscles to get that desk erected."

What?

Did she just say 'erect'?

Courtney's mind really started playing tricks on him after that statement, but he tried to stay cool.

"Don't change up your style now," he told himself, "just play it cool. Keep your swagger."

"Swagger? Yeah—swagger,"he thought, "I think thats what the youngsters are saying nowadays."

He tried to act like he didn't hear her.

"Courtney... I mean... Mr. Peterson. Would you like anything to drink?" she finally asked again, "I've got tea, soda, cold water or cold beer."

He had settled on a cold beer.

As she exited to go get it, of course he looked... couldn't help it. Couldn't help but to notice that twitch in her hips as she swayed out either.

Courtney was a mess.

"I wonder if she's doing that on purpose?" was his internal question that somehow longed for an external answer from her.

September returned.

"Hope you don't mind import?" she asked extending out a *Heineken*.

"Love 'em," he answered.

The desk construction was almost complete. He still had a little ways to go with it but as he continued Courtney wondered and questioned in his mind if he should end the night or the project by accepting a payment if she should ask.

Twenty bucks?

Should he even take it? Of course not. What if she should offer to take him out for a quick bite to show him her appreciation? Surely she'd be grateful *and* she had manners. So what should he do? He wondered. But before any answers could completely manifest themselves...

"I hope you don't mind but while you're finishing that, I'm gonna take a shower and get out of these work clothes."

September's one bedroom apartment was a small one. *And* it was the kind where the bathroom was actually still a part of its bedroom. She had rambled through a drawer or two to gather up some items that she would need and then took them into the bathroom with her before closing the door behind herself.

Courtney paid no attention to her as he labored on unitl he was done with the desk... and the imported beer.

At first he just sat there kind of in a daze or daydream like state as he listened to September's shower run.

"She was just on the other side of that door," he thought to himself, *"...naked."*

She was rubbing and caressing her body. Suds were bubbling and rolling over her

breast and cascading on down to her most
sensual and private body parts.

Courtney could imagine it all. He felt
himself getting ex-cited... and then the
sound stopped.

The water had been shut off.

Just as he heard the sound of the shower
curtain rings being pulled back across the
length of the metal shower curtain rod he
stood up and briskly walked toward the
living room. There he took a seat.

As soon as he did his cell phone rang.
September must've heard it and rushed out,
actually too prematurely, of the bathroom
and into the living room in efforts to warn
him and remind him not to tell Josh that he
was there... because remem-ber, "*it was
supposed to be a surprise.*"

But the problem was... she was still
dripping wet with only a towel wrapped
around her otherwise naked body.

"Don't tell Josh," she whispered standing
before Courtney.

But it was Belinda.

Well...why not tell her?

The surprise was for Josh, not her. Still
Courtney didn't breathe a word to her
concerning his whereabouts.

But again, why?

Courtney closed the flip on his cell phone and even if it was only for an instant of a second he still stared at September who weirdly enough didn't apologize for her near nakedness in his presence.

The ride home was awkward, disturbing, distant, and scary even.

Courtney didn't feel like himself. Maybe he was having an out of body experience or something while sitting in his passenger seat watching as someone else drove him home because this was some other guy. Some lustful old dude who was somehow getting caught up with thoughts of sleeping with his own son's girlfriend which was his soon to be daughter-in-law, *let us not forget.*

"Humph," he gestured pulling into his driveway.

He knew that he'd have to control himself on this one. Not only that, he'd have to stay away from this girl.

But with the couple's dinner coming up, the wedding and reception, how could he do that?

She'd be there and he'd *have* to be there. There was no way that he could miss any event now...not with what all had happened after he missed the night that Josh had proposed to her.

So Courtney vowed to stay strong.

He'd attend everything but he'd keep his distance.

That's probably the best for everyone.

THE LEFTHAND…THIRD FINGER

Re-cep-tion (ri sep' shan) n. 1. (a) a receiving or being received (b) the manner of this
2. a social function for the receiving of guests

Chapter Four

Everything went well.
The rehearsal, the rehearsal dinner, the wedding… and now, the reception.

The crowd received the freshly married couple now known as the *younger* Petersons with warmth and great cheer. Everyone was there even Ron C, Josh's boss from his job.
"Who would've ever thought that you two would've been the ones who got married? I remember the first day you guys met," he told them. "That was about how long ago?"
"About a hundred pounds ago, wasn't it?," Josh joked com-menting on Ron's tremendous weight loss.
But he looked good…and September told him so.
Everyone just loved that girl.
She was special and no one had any problems in telling Josh that and in letting him know just how lucky they thought he

was to have her. Even the minister had commented on how blessed he thought Josh was to have such a sweet wife.

"Thanks," Josh told the man of the cloth as he smiled and winked at his bride

The gifts were plentiful. The food delicious. The drinks maj-orly consumed. And the music...loud.

The time came for the father-in-law to dance with the bride.

"Go on out there!" everyone shouted.

Courtney smiled but refused as long as he could but there was no quieting and no satisfying the urging crowd until he obliged.

"Man, get your butt out there and dance with your daughter-in-law," Belinda demanded as she stood behind him smiling.

She happily gave Courtney a little shove and he was off...off to meet the woman that he had been dodging for so long in the middle of the dance floor.

Everyone looked and cheered on. From the sober ones...to the tipsy ones...to the all out drunk ones.

People were enjoying themselves. They truly enjoyed seeing these two generations of Petersons embrace and go forth in their steps toward bridging an old gap through this new union.

"You were acting like you were scared to come dance with me," September said barely audible over the loud music.

"Of course not," Courtney answered with a smile, "why would you say that?"

"Oh...I'm just saying."

They maneuvered through a slow song and covered as much ground as possible. It seemed to Courtney that the vocalist had already been singing forever. Sadly he was only halfway through the damn song. Courtney was ready to get off of that floor... *NOW!*

But time had slowed down. Actually, it had slowed down too damn much because he was beginning to feel something coming on. And it was an old *familiar* feeling. A feeling that Courtney really didn't need to be feeling right now.

"Oh my God," he said to himself as the feeling grew stronger and *harder.*

"So what do you want me to call you now?" September asked looking into hie eyes, " Daddy... or Big Daddy?"

"Huh?" Courtney asked being caught off guard. He felt his arousal.

"But how in the hell could he get an erection at a time like this?" he asked hisself.

"Come on, Courtney...stop tripping. I feel that thang that you keep rubbing up against my thigh. After tonight I'm gonna start calling you Big Daddy. Okay?"

"Aw, man," Courtney was now thinking, "if this song were to end now and she were to just walk away from me and leave me hanging in this condition it would be all over for me for sure. There'd be no way I could hide or explain this."

But look...

Funny how only minutes earlier that Courtney was ready for the song to end. But not anymore. Courtney's mind had changed. He no longer felt in a rush to get off that dance floor. Infact, he wanted to make it last forever…like Keith Sweat. Or better yet, like R. Kelly... atleast not until after his *own* needle had a chance to go down.

THE LEFTHAND...THIRD FINGER

*Af-fair (a fer') n. 1. a thing to do
2. matters of business
3. any matter, event, etc.
4. an amorous episode*

Chapter Five

Five Weeks Later

"And what if someone was to see us?" she was asking.

"See us doing what?" Courtney asked, "we're not doing anything --yet. Besides, what's wrong with a man spending time or riding in a car with his daughter?"

"Daughter-*in*-law," she corrected him with emphasis.

It had only been weeks since the wedding and now Courtney and September found themselves spending more and more time together... in a sneaky kind of way.

The guilty feeling had long passed for Courtney and as far as he could see September wasn't having too much of a problem with it herself. Well--other than the fact of acting a little nervous every time they stopped at a signal light.

"When are we gonna finally get off of these streets and spend some real time together?" she pressed and had asked him.

Courtney wished that he could answer that question...but he couldn't.

Though it was rather fun...the idea, just thinking of getting a room and having sex with this young tender was one thing. But the actuality of it becoming real somewhat nerved him. Not because of her age...or *his*.

Courtney was a good looking man and in the course of his historic run of cheating on Belinda there had been plenty of women ranging from various ages...some even the same age *as* September.

But he was nerved about this one because of *who* she was and who they'd be hurting if someone were to ever find out...*though he hoped that no one would.*

But why hadn't he been able to control his desires? What pushed him... or drew him in?

Glancing over at September the latter was obvious. He saw what drew him in. The sexiness that she possessed. Her legs, her thighs, her breast, the way that her jeans fitted so snug and revealing-like in her crotch area when she sat. Her voice when she'd call him...or when she answered his call. Or the way that she'd sit with her back against the passenger door and just stared at him as he drove.

It all drove him wild and mad with lust. But Courtney wanted the feelings to be neutral. He wanted to feel that someone else was guilty other than just himself.

Tonight he pulled over into the parking lot of an *Applebee's* and they got out. Inside, as they enjoyed laughter and good food, Courtney couldn't help but wonder with all the people there, who would actually know him? Hopefully not a soul.

He'd driven for miles, clear across town to a different side of the city in order to *not* be recognized.

Courtney tried hiding his concern but one can only hide darting eyes for so long.

"What's wrong?" September asked with a knowing smile, "it looks like you're trying to hide or something."

"Oh… that's funny, huh?" he asked.

And if he was hiding something, then he damn well knew of his guilt and it surely damn well was *quite* pitiful.

September's phone rang.

"Hello…" she answered.

She spoke briefly into it as Courtney looked on. He could tell who it was. It was Josh on the other end. Through each bite and fork full of food that went into his mouth he studied September's every move. But he couldn't hear her. She spoke lowly and softly into her handset. It was bad enough that they were already surrounded by a restaurant full of loud feasting people but now here she was being all *lovey-dovey* and private too.

It bothered Courtney.

When he made a gesture to her like, *"what's going on?"* She stretched her arm out towards him with her phone in her hand. "Here," she said with a serious look upon her face.

Courtney all but choked.

His eyes grew as wide as silver dollars which had he thought about it he would've doubted if September even knew what they were…considering her age. Silver dollars had basically become extinct. But he slowly reached out to take the phone anyway.

"He wants to talk to you," she told him. *"Me?...Shit!!"*

"Hello?" Courtney answered attempting to at least sound as normal and as innocent as possible.

But no one spoke.

"Hello?" he asked again but as before still no one answered.

At just that moment September burst out into laughter.

"You should've seen your face!" she spurted barely being able to control herself and her laughter.

But it wasn't funny. Not to Courtney...not at all.

In fact, he was mad as hell. And understandably enough--hell, Courtney had even lost his appetite.

"That *sh*...," Courtney had started almost including one of his always available 4-letter words before lowering his voice, "was not funny at all."

September sipped from a large soft drink.

"It was to me," she said rolling her eyes.

That look and that comment...surprised Courtney. He had never saw that nor that side of her.

With the confirmation of what was going on now resting deep within herself she had a different type of behavior it seemed for the whole remainder of their *date*.

By his actions he *knew* that he was involved in and doing something wrong. But he was in it too deep. There'd be no turning back from this point. Everything had to be played out *and* if she had to, she'd take it all the way to the bed.

THE LEFT HAND...THIRD FINGER

*De-cep-tion (de sep 'shan) n. 1. a deceiving
or being deceived
2. an allusion or fraud.*

Chapter Six

After that last episode Courtney had
refused to be seen in a public place like that
again with September... *any* public place.
   Yes, he had picked her up on occasion and
rode with her around town behind tint a
couple of times. He had even dropped a few
hundred dollars for an outfit or two. But
another restaurant...*hell no.*
   Courtney had damn near suffered a heart
attack that last time. He was already tripping
about being surrounded by people who
might've recognized him out there and then
she had to go and add that sick ass joke.
Nope, no more open public for them. In-fact,
why not just call everything off.

A Few Days Later

   "I've got something to talk to you about,"
he told her over the phone.

"Tell me now," she urged, "tell me, Courtney…What?…You don't want me no more? Is it because we ain't had sex yet?"

Her words and her questions were coming too fast.

Words, questions, accusations…everything.

Courtney didn't think that such a simple statement would bring about so much from her. It was a snowball effect. Things just kept rolling off of her tongue non stop. Courtney had to cut things off and end the conversation.

"We'll talk tomorrow," he told her.

"Tomorrow?" she asked. " No, let's talk now. Come over. Josh won't be home from work until later on. We have at least 3 or 4 hours to talk and to be together."

Courtney fought and struggled with it but his rational mind, if it could be called that, told him that *now* was the time. He'd have to take this opportunity to go over and call things off. It was the perfect chance. It was what had to be done.

Thirty minutes later

September's front door slowly swung open allowing Courtney's entrance. He looked at her. Had she been crying? Was it really that serious? She locked the door behind him.

Courtney stood there waiting on her to hug him or something but after locking the door she stepped around him and walked on into the kitchen quickly returning with a bottle opener and two beers.

"Here," she said handing everything to Courtney, "you need one of these... I sure as hell do."

He took everything, opened the first one and handed it to her. And then he took the second one, his own, and opened it.

Now sitting on the couch with her opposite of him he noticed again how sad she was looking. It wasn't until now that it registered to him that she was wearing a robe...whether anything was underneath it or not he didn't know nor did he care to find out.

He had came here for a reason.

"We can't go on like this," Courtney said getting right to the point, "it was a mistake that never should've happened and I realize that now. I'm sorry for even letting it get this far. I love my wife and I..."

"And I love my husband!" September interrupted in an almost scream, "but this ain't about them. This ain't about Josh, Belinda, or me either! This is about you, Courtney!"

September had almost spilled something. She took a breath, calmed herself down, and continued.

Raising herself from the couch now and easing her way toward Courtney with an intimate voice she softly and sexually said, "this is about you playing games with me and my emotions."

Whoa...she was coming closer.

By now Courtney could see her robe loosening up as it began falling from her body. Her breast were visible now.

"Playing with your emotions?" he asked now feeling the weight of her body upon his.

She had already taken the beers from him and sat them on the floor.

"Yeah, you heard me-- playing with my emotions. I knew that you wanted me... and I want you too. But just because I couldn't just rush and jump into bed with you... now you wanna leave me alone?"

"Nah, that's not it, baby."

"Baby? Oh...now I'm *baby*?"

September was working on Courtney and doing a hell of a good job at it. Courtney didn't know if he was coming or going.

He felt himself getting aroused as she pressed more firmly against him. She could feel him too now. She kissed at his lips.

"September," he tried to say but her tongue caught him.

He fought.

"Wait --hold on--wait a minute," he demanded.

Courtney struggled to break free and to get on his feet, "what the hell are you doing?"

"I'm doing what you want me to do, Courtney. I'm ready. You can have me now. Don't you want me? Don't you want *this*?"

The robe fell completely.

Courtney's stare started at the base of her feet where the robe had gathered and worked its way up. She stood there unashamed and bare. Courtney had to reach down and grab his beer.

Damn...

Now as he downed the rest of it while taking in the vision that stood before him he realized that it was his desires that had brought him here and that his hopes were that when he'd threated to break things off that she'd do just this.

Courtney seemed happy all over again.

But why? Had he forgotten...*again*?

"Why don't we go into the room?" he suggested.

September did as she was told and from that point on everything else was done as Courtney had directed.

The look upon her face said that she was scared.

"But don't be scared now," Courtney thought to himself, "you're the one that started all this."

He told her to lay upon the bed… *she did.*
He stood over her as he undressed himself… *she watched.*
He climbed upon her sheets… *she trembled.*

And then he touched her.
Slowly he caressed her thighs and parted them. It took him giving a little push at first but eventually they were open.

Do you want this? *She said nothing.*
Do you like this? *Still no word.*
Can I kiss you here? *He did.*

Courtney's head disappeared.
So deep was his lust and so insatiable was his desire that the sounds of her faint weeping and the tears of her present pain escaped him. He heard nothing.
September pulled and grabbed at the pillow that was behind her head and began screaming into it… "No! No! No!"
But Courtney couldn't hear her. He was *too involved… too busy… too everything.*
He felt her shake… but thought that she was cumming.

Heard her cry… but thought that it was ecstasy.

And then…he heard the sound of a gunman's click behind his ear.

"Josh!" September cried.

As Josh held the gun tears streamed down his face.

After all these years it had come to this. He couldn't believe it. Out of all the women in this city Courtney had to chase after the wrong one…

"Mine!" Josh had yelled.

Courtney's heart raced. His hands were up and outstretched before his son. September's eyes were still filling with tears. She couldn't stop crying because she knew what would be the out-come.

"Why Dad?" Josh asked with trembling hands.

"Son, I..."

"Why!" his son demanded again.

Josh raised the gun once more but this time when he did he did it with an intent set so deep within the souls of his eyes that it shook Courtney.

"Please, son… don't," his father begged now trying to calm himself *and* his son down.

"Please son, don't what? Say it! Beg you bastard!"

"Don't…," he started and then dropped his head, "don't do this," he tried to say but the words got caught up in his throat as he, too, began to cry.

Time stood still.

Josh tightened his finger around the trigger that now felt as cold as ice. He fought to aim.

"Son, I love you."

"Love me? If you did you wouldn't have been trying to sleep with me wife."

"But, son… I'm sorry."

"Yeah-- you've been sorry since the day you started hitting my mama!"

Darkness surrounded a light that quickly became replaced by a vacuum as Josh's anger and pain suddenly reduced itself into a smell of gun powder that quickly overtook the conditioned air of the room.

He had pulled the trigger.

No one dare moved…or breathed for all that mattered.

Silence demanded its respect and respect demanded its reign.

"911?" Josh asked speaking into his cell phone.

"Yes sir…what is your emergency?"

"I just killed my father."

THE LEFTHAND…THIRD FINGER

The Final Chapter

The police came.
The medical team came
The investigators came.
The coroner's office came.
Belinda came.
The media came.
People from around the apartment complex
came.
Tears came.
Screams came.
Questions came.
More questions came…and more questions
followed.

And then the handcuffs.

The arrest came.
The book in came.
The finger printing came.

The photo… *face front… now turn sideways.*
The small cell.

The investigators... again...and another interrogation.

And then a statement from Josh Peterson... the only one he had made.

"I want to talk to my lawyer."

The case was manslaughter but Josh's lawyer pleaded that it was temporary insanity.

The terms and the legal jargon were confusing but it was also plain to see that it was a *crime of passion.*

So... did the jury understand?

Were they compassionate towards the fact that this was this guy's own father's death that he was being tried for?

"For crying out loud..." his lawyer shouted, "this young kid hasn't even had a chance to have a decent mourning phase for his father!"

But he was countered by the prosecuting attorney.

"Father?" he asked. "Yeah well I doubt if he was telling his dad how much he was going to miss him while he has pumping him full of slugs, Counselor!"

The comment had to be stricken from the record but everyone still heard it loud and clear...it had hit home with the jury.

"Did he deserve to be murdered?" ...*yelled the prosecutor.*

"Did *she* deserve to be raped?" ... *the defendant's lawyer shot back quickly.*

"She was a woman who had consented!" ...*informed the prosecutor.*

"No...she was a *girl* who had been manipulated!"

The state's prosecutor stepped around from his table and began walking toward the jury.

"Well," he began, "I have credit card receipts in which my legal team has researched and investigated that has placed this *young lady in question* in the company of Mr. Peterson on *various occasions* at *various locations* as they rendezvoused throughout the city during their many *'consented'* dates."

Josh's lawyer objected arguing that one could hardly classify a moment of lunch or dinner spent between a young lady and her *father-in-law* as a date...claiming that the younger Mrs. Peterson was merely trying to work her way into a major dysfunctional family while at the same time reconstruct and rebuild a much needed bridge between the father and his son... her husband.

"She seduced him!" the prosecutor raged.

"No, don't be fooled... she feared him!"

And then…the secret weapon.

It was definitely something that the DA's office didn't want the public nor the jury to see…**THE RECORDING.**

"A what? A DVD?" they had first asked.

Yes…a DVD. Something had been caught on tape.

"Who was the recording of and where did it come from?"

The answer was from some type of camera or web cam set up on a computer that was sitting on a desk directly across from the couple's bed.

It had been set up in a corner, they had added.

In the corner?

Well, who set the camera up?

The recording had showed an older man gesturing to a younger scared looking lady to lie on the bed. It appeared that she had only done what she was told. He then undressed *himself* without any of her help. So…to anyone viewing the video, it was clear that she didn't want to be there because there wasn't any involvement from her at all. And again, the look upon her face was fear.

The Jury Listened As They Watched

"And then this *adulterer*," Josh's lawyer narrated , "forced her to open her legs stealing the young girl's very essence all the while as he defiled his own son's bed of sacred vows. Can't you see her tears? She's screaming into her pillow for him to stop. Stop this madness! Don't make me do this! Please…someone help me."

And someone did… her husband.

The monster's son came to her rescue. His father… *her* father-in-law.

The courtroom bled of silence.

The jury all but cried with the girl ashamed of themselves for even *forcing* her to relive the moment. She was there. Yeah, September was there alongside her grieving husband to support *him* not even withstanding her own piercing pain.

And Belinda was there too… fighting the sins of Josh's father, and as she fought them she fought them by holding back tears…by sitting beside her daughter-in-law as they both sat square shouldered and chin up…and by looking at and staring every single jurist directly in their eyes with a message that said, "It's okay…go ahead and do your job. I understand."

And they did.

It took only 15 minutes of deliberation before the jury returned with a 'NOT GUILTY' verdict.

But who had lost? Who had won? And whose life could go on as normal now? No one's. Life had dealt a terrible hand.

THE LEFTHAND...THIRD FINGER

The Epilogue

The gray skies lasted long. But those
skies had been gray over Josh's head for
many years... and they carried weight.
But since his acquittal he hadn't felt that
weight. He hadn't felt weight...or anger...or
sadness...*or* depression.
He felt light.
He could even feel the sun now as it
shined down on him encouraging him to go
on. Go forward. Live again.
Did he need more time to mourn? Had he
had enough time yet?

And what about his mom? Well...

Belinda visited often--her husband's
grave and her son's home.
She explained to him how important it was
to cry and told him how unhealthy is was for
him *not* to cry.
"Don't hold it in," she told him, "I haven't
seen you shed not one single tear since your
dad's death."
And he hadn't. And he wasn't. Truth
was...he and his wife had put all of the past

behind. They were the new Petersons--a couple who, in such a short time, had already been through it all.

They had been through so much.

But today Josh is thinking back.

"Was it was worth it?"

"Damn right it was," he answered September as they both looked at the insurance company's beneficiary check that paid off Courtney's policy.

September had came at the right time in Josh's life. And he *knew* that she was the type of chick that his dad would fall for.

Again...Josh had waited a long time for this woman.

She was perfect.

Booty...Beauty...and Brains

Together they came clean.

"So, how did you know that I'd go along with your plan to kill your father, Josh?"

"I didn't," he told her, "I was just hoping that you would."

Back Story

Josh began hating Courtney from the very first time that he witnessed him hitting his mom. As a child it confused him and it traumatized him. Not only was this his mother but this was also the mother that he loved and the woman who had nursed him, and raised him, and played with him, and kissed all his boo-boos.

And this was also the woman that Courtney was supposed to have loved also...forever. But he didn't. Didn't even try as far as what Josh had seen. Not since he was a child

Josh was sure that it didn't start out that way. Hey, afterall...let's not forget that these two started out as high school sweethearts. But as Josh got older he begin taking notice in his parents arguments...and in the things that were said.

And then he got even older...

And he found out that Courtney was a liar.

He was a liar...he cheated...he lied when he got caught cheating...and he was a WIFE BEATER.

Maybe he and Belinda could've worked out things with everything else, but the hidden bruises...the obvious heavy make-up...the occasional dark sunglasses.

Didn't take a genius.

But as time went by Josh had even tried to forgive his father...for his mother's sake, ofcourse.

He tried to forgive him, love him, and he tried to go forward. But Courtney kept going *backwards. Kept forcing pain and shame upon the family, until...one day Josh made up his mind.*

He decided it and he made a Blood Pact within himself as he vowed to do to Courtney what Courtney had done to his mother. But as you could figure, Courtney kept topping each last screw up with one better every time until just a good ol' fashion ass whipping and beat down wouldn't have been good enough...Courtney deserved worse.

Joshua Peterson began saving up for a lawyer when he was 12yrs old...cutting lawns, trimming trees, saving his allowances, and anything else in the way of odd jobs that would make him money.

Anything other than selling drugs or doing something illegal, ofcourse.

You see...Joshua Peterson knew that in order for his plan to be successful: meaning, for him make it out of the whole ordeal squeaky clean... he would have had to live 'the perfect life'. He could not have chanced it. Stepping into a court room on charges of Felony Murder with priors? No way.

At 16...he lied about his age and took out a Life Insurance Policy on his dad and paid the premium faithfully until the day of execution.

For over 10yrs he had been successfully planning, plotting, and orchestrating his whole plan...and then he met September. Wow! Was it love at first sight? Not by far. Joshua only felt that it was getting close to time. He wasn't rushing anything but Courtney wasn't letting up any either. And again...September was the perfect lure. Couldn't have gotten one better.

Courtney at times would have those father-son talks about things such as integrity and morals and stuff like that...but he had none. And Josh knew it.

Given the right timing, the right setting, the right opportunity, and the right person...Josh knew that Courtney would fail the ultimate test. He had even did a trial run with him by having September call to have him come set up a desk at her apartment...that same desk that Josh's computer and web cam had sat upon on that tragic day.

Ironically, and sadly so, Courtney had set his own deathtrap.

But it was all over now.

No more arguments. No more beatings. No more other women. And no more life insurance premium payments. Josh had

*beaten the system, already gotten his check,
and now they were the 'new' Petersons.
They would take that money and start their
new lives with it.*

*September eyed her husband now as their
conversation began winding down and
coming to a close.
She studied him
Had he been cold blooded in his actions?
Could there have been a different
outcome?
Why did she even agree and why did she
let Josh use her?
Didn't matter…she was just as guilty now.
But she had questions as she stood knowing
that their secret could never be found out.*

"Did you hate him that much?" she asked
him.

"Yeah…I did," he answered dryly.

"And so you allowed him to come after
me, huh?"

"No…I didn't allow him to come after
you, September. He *chose* to."

The End

Saving the last Dancer

By A.e. Santi

You are now entering in to another story.

Book Three

Saving the Last Dancer

Chapter One

She was his yin.

He was her yang.

She never knew him...but even if she had known that he existed it was not notice enough that she had cared.

But he had noticed her.

Every day he saw her at her locker just smiling and carrying on with those other popular girls that hung around with her.

He played in the band.

She-- well, she just played.

Being the tuba player his place was so far back in the rear of the band behind all the other brass and woodwinds, that feeling buried, he'd just accept the fact in life that she wasn't going to be the one for him. Not in this lifetime.

"It probably wouldn't work anyway," he told himself but all the while borderline fantasizing and secretly hoping that somehow it could work.

And the girl could dance!

Damn that girl could dance.

She and her crew would always wait until just the right amount of people would arrive and get together in the school's auditorium, gym or any other place or venue that welcomed high school events and then they'd burst right into their dance routines and rock the hell out of a crowd.

They'd turn a party out.

They'd be crunk!

It would be girls going wild, guys going crazy, music up loud and them shaking their asses all the way toward junior stardom.

It was teenage life at its best. Fun to the fifth power. And that was Karla Dancer... 15 years ago. And that was me too.

I never knew what happened to her. Just like I never made it to be some big time music producer or video *genius* either.

I had promised myself that had I did, I'd find her and have her right there center stage, bright lights and all, shaking all that ass...grown woman style-- but minus her home girls.

I probably would've married her too. You know, had some kind of Jay Z/ Beyoncé type thing going on.

But I didn't. Instead I went from the marching band uniforms to military dress uniforms.

Chapter Two

I enlisted.
I did my tour.
I saw combat.

I saw death, I lost friends, and I
experienced fear... *real fear.*
Not just any type of fear like the kind
you come down with when the cops get
behind you and start following you.
Or, let's take it up a notch... when you've
got tickets, warrants, a blunt, a gun *and*
drugs in the car with you and the cops get
behind you and start following you...with
their lights on. Now that's fear.
But that's still not good enough.
That's nothing. Nothing compared to
wondering and fearing that as you
stumble to remember the Lord's prayer in
hopes of saving your *own* ass even while
stuffing half of your hand and fingers into
a hole in the center of your new best
friend's torso that's the size of your
grandfather's old baseball. All this as

bullets larger than the size of any ghetto hood approved *choppa* can throw at you. As bullets whizz by the both of your heads. ...you *fear* that you're going to die... you *fear* that you'll never make it back home again alive...nor get a chance to see your mother's. girlfriends, son's, or daughter's face again. You also *fear*, like with your last two bullet-ridden dead best friends, that this one don't look up at you with a mouth full of spurting blood and ask you to promise him that you won't let him die. And again, while trying to save your own ass.

Yeah, that's fear.

But fear or not...I fought, endured and finally made it home.

Surprisingly to no *real* fanfare.

There was no girlfriend, no son, no daughter...never knew my dad, so he was out--and because of that one official government financed dreadful phone call a little more than two years earlier... no mother either.

But made it home, I did.

And I was thankful...at first. At least until the reality of being there hit me. And when it did, it hit me just as hard as one of those runaway battlefield slugs would have. Thank God, it caused less damage. I was still alive.

But home or what I called home wasn't the only thing that had changed. *I* had changed. Maybe it was because of the war or the exposure to seeing people's heads blown off. Or their arms, or legs, or whatever. I had seen it all. Enough to know that I wasn't normal anymore.

So, me being different now I guess I saw the streets differently as well. I tasted blood in the air now.

I saw through the dealers who stood on the corners as they peddled whatever drug that had became the popular highs of the month. Whether it was crack, cocaine, ice, OG Cush...*handle bars* or whatever. They were nothing, and all that *hardness* that they were portraying in front of all them people that they were preying on...was bullshit. All of that would've died right out there with them if they were out there in those war zones where I was.

I became enraged with hate every time *anyone* in *any type* of traffic would somehow accidentally or purposely cut me off, slow down in front of me, look at me crazy, toot their horn, leave their blinker on too long, or well... hell, did anything at all that I didn't like. For some reason, cut and dry, I just wasn't a *people's person* anymore.

Sad... but it slowly began dawning on me that not only did I *not* like anyone anymore, but it was clear also that for some reason or another I actually preferred that they all just died.

Saving the Last Dancer

Chapter Three

Again, I'm not a genius and neither did it take me long to figure out what I wanted to do now that I was back home from war... and it didn't take long for me to conclude my decision.

After so many years of *me* fighting to stay alive or trying to keep someone else alive it had finally boiled down to the fact that I just didn't care anymore.

For years without me realizing it the military had been honing and programming me to be good at one thing only after they were done with me, and that was killing.

While there I had remained on the stock end of a rifle for so long that now it would only feel natural, even if I wasn't in the military anymore. I was in the civilian world now...and it was jacked up. I hated it. And it made me still feel the urge to *Kill The Enemy.*

But I was determined not to become some sort of vigilante type self-righteous motherfucker that slithered through the city's streets at night in hopes of finding some poor un-suspecting misfortunate soul moonlighting his way through college tuitions or daycare fees.

I wasn't happy about what was going on in the hoods, but truthfully... I wasn't really *that* fucked up about it either. I got over it and eventually had taken on the attitude of *fuck it, let the dead bury their own.*

If I did it... I wanted money. I had to get paid for mine.

So I went through the proper channels of getting my name out there and letting my profession be known. I put my P.O.C. (*Point of Contact*) in all the right publications and on any web sites in social media that mattered.

After that, I just sat back and waited.

And I Waited Some more

The first call that came through my new untraceable *busi-ness* phone was from a hysterical and suspecting housewife who was convinced that her husband was cheating on her. Hence... she wanted *him* and that *stripper bitch*, her words, dead.

"I want you to cut the freaking emergency brake cable and drain his master cylinder until it's as dry as the old geezer's nut sack... and then, make it look like an accident!"

"What!"

It took damn near an hour's worth of my limited minutes trying to explain to her that *that* would not make it look like an accident. The only resulting death would come from him backing out of his own driveway unbeknownst of his premeditated mechanical disposition and clumsily crashing into their across-the-street neighbor's mailbox...thus murdering *it* only.

She hung up the phone in my face.

I spent the following days trying to come up with a signature name... something catchy. Something that sounded *like* something. A name that I could build a reputation upon.

Using my real name was out of the question, but what about a nickname deriving from it or close to it?

My name is Federick Upchurch... so how about Fed Up?

Hell no!

That sounded like a joke or something and this was some serious business.

I was a hitman now... a hired gun...an assassin, and long ago had my smiles worn thin.

I chose the name Beckmon.

Why Beckmon? I have no idea, but since it popped up I just went with it. It sounded good. One word, two syllables... real easy.

First Real Call

"This is Beckmon," I answered the phone.

"I need to meet with you," the male's voice said.

"Who is this?"

"Who am I? I'm your next three paychecks," he ans-wered,"...with an advance."

"How'd you get this number?" I asked in a catechizing manner hoping that he'd come back with the right answer...and he did.

An hour later we were sitting across the table from one another in an expensively decorated downtown restaurant sharing what some would call *war stories*.

This guy had retired from killing... me, I never stopped.

He was seeking out a new talent for his client...me, I was as new as they came.

He said that I was green...me, I convinced him that I was *raw*.

Without even once touching or sipping from his $300 a bottle glass of wine during our entire conversation the man who had introduced himself to me simply as *Michael*...no last name, then slid two envelopes across the table to me. One was the contract with all related information; pictures, addresses, etc. Number two's envelope was $50,000.

"Enjoy your lunch, Mr. Beckmon," Michael had said as he rose from the table bringing into view the remainder of what appeared to be a very expensive and tailored suit.

I took notes.

Thirty minutes later I was sitting in my car, a 2008 Cadillac Deville, staring at three black-and-white photos of my first job.

It was a man. His name was Stacey Pratt.

At first glance everything about the man told me that he was a drug dealer.

Ok...easy job.

An even quicker glance at my intel and fact sheet informed me of his whereabouts... Arlington, Texas. He was hiding out at a friend's house (*probably someone who he'd been feeding dope to keep quiet*).

But they didn't. They sold him out. He was found 3 hours later lying dead on the middle of his so-called friend's kitchen floor. One single shot through a window over the sink. One entrance wound in and one out through the center of his forehead.

Stacey Pratt had been rinsing an apple off when he thought that he had seen a flash or something that had come from the rooftop of a neighboring house across a large field to the rear of his friend's home.

Well, he did. But it was from the sun's glare off the lenses of my power scope as I dialed up my minutes and adjusted my weapon for windage.

Everything that I had learned from my military instructor at my old scout and sniper school and, even later on reminded of by my team leader while in war instantly came back to my mind.

"Always shoot on empty lungs!" one of the guys had instructed me.

"Keep a steady pull on the trigger," the other would say, "even after the round leaves the barrel."

Through my scope I saw him enter the kitchen. Then he stepped out of view. Seconds later there he was again in my crosshairs. I imagined myself back in the Middle East and Pratt being Hadji, which is what Charlie was to Vietnam.

And then... *BANG!*

Center. Good hit.

"A man who gets the job done," Michael said over the phone, "I commend you, Beckmon because there are alot of slackers out there."

But I wasn't in the mood for small talk and Michael being more experienced than I had thought that he was im-mediately picked up on it.

"First civilian kill?" he asked.

I cursed myself for being so obvious and transparent.

"I'm good," I lied, "what's next?"

"Hey listen...the guy was scum," he added, "don't let it bother you."

"Michael, I said I'm Good... so again, what's next?"

"We're looking for something," he told me, "I'm waiting on my guys to finish up with the clean-up job. If it comes up zilch--you and I meet again."

"And if they find it?" I asked now approaching the borderline of me probably sounding antsy. I was hoping that Michael didn't pick up on it.

When he first called me he introduced himself to me as my next *three* paychecks. I was beginning to see those last two slipping away.

"Then it'll all be over," he said, "and we'll all go back to our normal lives."
And the line went dead after that. But normal? My life could never be normal again.

I spent the next few hours watching TV and surfing through channels. By 11 o'clock there still wasn't any mention of a death, a murder, a body found...nothing.

I was convinced that Michael's little clean-up crew had done a good job. A damn good job... so for me, there was nothing to worry about.

However, I wasn't worried... I was bothered.

But bothered by what? Not about the fact that I had just killed a man, but about the fact that I had just killed a man and that it *didn't* bother me.

After powering off the TV I slipped into my bedroom, put my money underneath my mattress and buried my head deep within my pillow.

Sleep came easy.

Chapter Four

As I Slept

"We won that one!" my homeboy way yelling giving out a high five.

"Them busters ain't got nothing on us!" one of my other friends answered.

We were in high school and although I was dreaming I was excited and rushing to get out of my band uniform too.

My mom had given me the car keys to her Taurus but with a very strict 12 o'clock midnight curfew... and I had no time to waste.

All of my bandmates were crunk. Not because of our team winning the football game, because we didn't. We lost--them cats were sorry. But because we had just brought the house down during our annual *Battle of The Bands* showdown and had put our rivals to shame.

"I know them girls from West Tech gonna be there bopping around!" one of our band's star percussionist had shouted. It had earned him a round of "hell yeahs!" and a whole bunch of high fives.

But I could've cared less. I was rushing to get to one girl and one girl only... Karla Dancer.

And she was there too.

By the time that I had got to the McDonald's parking lot it was packed. Cars were everywhere, people were everywhere, but all I had to do was look for the liveliest circle of people and chances were she'd be right in the middle of it.

I fought my way to the front and made it there just in time to see her *drop it like it's hot*...with her ass toward me.

My night was complete. That was all I needed just to see and to watch her do her thing.

I wasn't a stalker...hell, I just didn't know how to approach her.

She and her girls were bringing their dance routine to a close. Somehow our eyes met as they all began walking my way.

"Maybe I should say something," I thought.

But before I could, Jaden *the superstar varsity quarterback juggernaut* stepped out of the crowd and walked up to her.

He was wearing his letterman's jacket. "You wanna ride with me through the Drive-Thru?" he asked her.

I wanted to shout to her, "No! He was on the losing team! *I'm* the tuba player ...and we won!"

But I didn't...never could see myself as being a hater.

But she surprised me.

"Nah...I'm cool," she said. "I'm hanging out with my home girls."

She crushed boy-wonder's ego and suddenly being a little scrawny sousaphone toting kid didn't seem so bad after all.

I woke up the next morning thinking about her and wondering *why* had I even dreamt about her.

Sure I was back in my old city but I hadn't thought about Karla in a while. Besides, she was so fast back then that either a miracle would've had to happen or by now she probably had *Baby Daddies* sprawled all over the city.

Either *that*, on drugs, or she was some Bishop Don Juan's Pimp'n Ass Nigga's bottom *ho*.

And none of that worked for me. I got up and took a shower.

I waited the whole day for a call that never came.

So...

I shopped.

Got my car detailed.

Got a manicure, haircut and was even tempted to get a pedicure...but I didn't.

Part of me claimed that as a hired gun now it made me feel soft. The other side blaming it on the ankle holster that I now wore everywhere.

I removed it for nothing and nobody. And having a pissed off pedicurist that close to my gun and that irritated by my feet was something that I preferred not to chance.

But that night I found myself sitting in front of a television screen again waiting on something that still never came.

I began the process of putting Michael and his people out of my mind. Seems my business with them had run its course. So, no longer should I be just sitting around waiting on their call. There were more fish out there to fry and with all the bait that I had thrown out there surely another one would be nibbling or biting at my line soon. Or, atleast I thought and hoped that they would.

Finally, my untraceable phone rang again.
"Beckmon," I answered.
"We need to meet again," I heard the smooth familiar voice say.
"Where?" I asked.
He told me.
"When?"
"In an hour."

It wasn't the same restaurant but its menu and interior décor were, if not as equivalent, probably more exquisite than that of our first meeting.

Michael was already there and had already been seated by the time that I'd got there. Word had been left with the maître d' to show me in. As he and I approached the table area I could see Michael standing to greet me.

He stretched his arm out and extended his hand to me.

"Mr. Beckmon," he greeted with a cordial gesture inviting me to have a seat, "please,,, it's nice that you are able to join me."

"Feelings are mutual, Michael. Thanks for having me," I answered hoping like hell that he had noticed my new suit.

And If he did he played it off quite well and never mentioned it, which I felt was a classy move.

Another pricey bottle of wine was brought out but this time we drank together.

Neither of us seemed big on small talk but this time I noticed the extra time spent on the basics, like...How have you been? ...Enjoying the city's nightlife? Need a girl or *two*... I can fix you up?

But things quickly grew quiet. Michael stared into space across the empty restaurant and then looked at me.

He took a breath, a swallow instead of a *sip* of his wine, and then another breath. Then he focused on everything about me that could be seen from where he sat. I wasn't even worried about my suit by this time. I could see that some-thing heavier was on his mind. It was in his eyes.

Again, I began feeling transparent but said nothing. I wait-ed and finally he spoke...it wasn't until days later that I had realized that the conversation that he had with me that day was one that was spoken directly to my soul.

"Things have turned difficult and we need someone whom we *know* can handle this next job, Beckmon."

I almost felt insulted. It was as if he was questioning my ability or my talent. Hell...and what about my results from that other job?

"So what are you saying, Michael?" I asked and added, " I completed that last..."

I lowered my voice more, "my last hit as instructed and I... "

"No, Mr. Beckmon," he interrupted, "it's not you.Though you *are* kind of green our concern lies more in the target than in you. Besides, on this particular job we'll be using more than just one gun anyway."

"What the hell did *'more than just one gun'* mean?" I thought without asking.

But I was sure that he'd tell me soon enough.

It was time for me to swallow now *and* pour, because by the look of things I was slowly beginning to hear my cash cow moo away toward greener pastures... and I just wasn't having that.

"I work alone," I stated and still remaining calm I added, "I don't do partners...nor teams."

"If you do choose to accept this job then you will be working alone, Mr. Beckmon.

But again, I'm telling you...things have turned difficult and no matter how it's handled there's going to be a lot of heat and hyped-up media coverage behind this one. We can't just make this one disappear into thin air like we've done a lot of the others," he explained.

"Why?" I asked, "isn't this one attached somehow and connected to that Pratt job that I did for you guys? I mean--I didn't see anything on the news or in the papers about him. Didn't your clean up guys make *that* disappear? What's so different about this one?"

"Listen, Beckmon... Pratt was trash. He was greedy, unpredictable, weak, flashy... not to mention, he knew too much."

"But he's dead now, Michael. Dead men can't talk," I said.

"Correct... but we're afraid that this one may have been babbling a long time before he even got to the grave."

Silence fell between us and a certain quietness took over me as I searched his eyes for an answer or a meaning to what he had just said. And remaining in thought, myself, I wondered about this next job. Who was it and why was it so difficult?

Michael ordered a second bottle of wine. No food had been ordered as of yet and it appeared that there wouldn't be. I searched the man's face for answers still. It was then that I first noticed the bags beneath his eyes. Puffiness that I had somehow missed before.

Were they there before or had this situation grown into such problem that even a man seemingly as cold as I had understood Michael to be became so affected to the point of losing that much sleep behind it?

Before our first *swallows* could be taken out of the new bottle of wine, with what appeared to be little struggle Michael unexpectedly hit me with the *who* and the *why*.

"What! A preacher!" I damn near shouted, "Michael... are you freaking serious?"

And he was.

"It's crazy I know. And that's why I said 'if you *choose* to accept this job'" he reminded me.

I killed a glass, poured a glass, refilled a glass (*his*) and damn-near hit up another glass for myself all at the same time. When I raised my glass again to go in for a second kill he stalled me.

"Easy Beckmon," he warned, "you might want to slow down. Unlike some wines, at $400 a bottle, these grapes just might sneak up on you when you least expect."

"Yeah... kind of like the wrath of God?" I asked sarcastically and down went the kill.

A preacher? A pastor of an almost 6,000 plus member mega church?

Are you serious?

I wasn't believing my ears. *This* was the target?

No, this wasn't the target...this was an express ticket to hell! And although I *knew* that there'd be consequences to my actions I wasn't exactly ready to face them this damn soon.

"Man... I hope you're not talking about," I lowered my voice almost to a whisper as if God couldn't hear...*yeah right,* "TD Jakes?" I finished.

Michael looked at me...scared me for a second.

"Ofcourse not... but there's more," he confessed.

I said nothing. I only stared at him like, "*come on with it.*"

"My people are requesting that the whole family be taken out. The mother and the father, too, along with the Pastor which is an only child. With the parents gone there'd be less chance of anyone else making noise or fuss about it after the case disappears from the headlines and out the limelight. Cold cases eventually become distant memories and faces forgotten."

"Yeah...until Judgment Day," I said .

Saving the Last Dancer

Chapter Five

Headed That Way...

Pastor Williams' church was even larger than I had ex-pected and although it claimed an almost 6,000 member ros-ter, its size clearly stated that a couple more thousand soul searching parishioners could have easily been added to its growing discipleship without a problem. Especially after being divided amongst the two mega services that were held each Sunday.

I glanced up at the church and then slid its picture back into an envelope. Then I pulled out a piece of paper that listed two addresses. I was sitting outside the first one but after one more look at the newer model black S-series Mercedes that sat in a spot with a sign in front of it that read: 'PLEASE DON'T TOW...THE PASTOR JUST STEPPED IN TO SEE JESUS', I slid my gearshift into drive and headed toward the second address.

"Nice neighborhood," I thought, "but nothing like what I'd thought it'd be."

The homes were large, well kept, and accented by beautifully landscaped lawns... but historic.

I had imagined something more modern. They were nice and colossal even. Most of them could've easily been valued at $400k or so if not a cool half a mil or more...but they weren't my style.

I thought about the houses. Then the car at the church. And then Stacey Pratt.

How could all of this have had something in common? And what was the story anyway? Michael hadn't offered an explanation...only a payment, which was fine with me.

I found the address and did a pass. All was quiet. There was a white Volvo wagon in the driveway and a newer model F-150 parked behind it...the parent's vehicles.

After finding a spot to park a block and a half away, I reached into my glove box and grabbed my .45 and silencer. I concealed them and took out walking in the direction of the pastor's house.

Again I noticed just how preserved looking this commun-ity really was. Old or not, it still was nice. Maybe good ol' Pastor Williams wanted to buy a decent home for himself that was still cool enough to move his aging parents into that would reflect their style and not conflict with his. That way it would still allow them to enjoy life and live comfortable together until their days ended (which because of me and the recent price tags hanging above their heads, would be today).

I rang the doorbell. No Answer.

I concentrated again on what I'd say when the door *was* answered. I was going to use a made up sob story about my wife's missing Shih Tzu requesting that if they did so happen to see "Lil Princess" would they please call me.

However, because I had so clumsily forgotten my business cards or anything to write with back in my car they'd have to walk off into their home to get an ink pen and paper thus leaving me out on their front door step so that once they turned the corner I'd come crashing right in behind them. *Or* they would stick with southern hospitality and invite me in. Either way they were a done deal. I was still getting in..

But still no answer.

Somehow my gut instincts began taking over as I began feeling like something just wasn't right. Something was wrong...I could feel it.

Too many vehicles were out front. I figured that more than likely the Volvo belonged to the Pastor's mom while the truck could've been the father's.

I began thinking.

Had they been here they would've answered by now. Had they rode somewhere together only one vehicle would be left behind? And had they rode with someone else, judging by the neighborhood, I'm almost sure that the cars would've been in the garage?

I looked around and down the street making sure that no one was watching and then I tried the door handle.

Nothing. It was locked.

After making my way around back I briskly stepped up onto the rear porch and reached for its doorknob.

I stopped short. It was a French door. A pane was broken and the door was ajar. I looked around again before pulling out my gun and attaching the silencer.

Four-five to my side I pushed the door open with my foot and went in. No one was in the kitchen. I began clearing the house. Halfway though it I began hearing a faint sound coming from a room off to my left. I quietly moved forward and closer. The sound was slightly louder but clearer now... and familiar.

I could hear the voices of people in unison almost singing the words "*good answer, good answer*". and now peeping around the corner...gun ready, I saw Steve Harvey.

Someone was watching Family Feud and I could see the back of their heads as they sat in their chairs facing an enormous flat screen.

But something was funny, I looked closer.

I counted two heads, two chairs... and then two bullet holes coming out the back of each chair.

"More than just one gun," I remember Michael saying.

They had already been here. Another assassin. Another gun.

My eyes quickly began scanning the area. Across the room something suddenly caught my attention.

A picture.

There were several. But the one with the flag... a uniform... and a badge *really* popped out at me. A police?...a cop? I stepped closer. The closer I got the more familiar the face got until...

"Jaden Williams? Jaden the freaking juggernaut-letterman- Williams?"

I raced toward the photograph. It *was* him. Jaden had be-came a police officer after we had graduated and although he looked older in this photo, it definitely was him.

Atop of the old upright standing piano, the picture jumped out and spoke to me it seemed. It beckoned me to stop, slow down, look, search, seek, find...do something. It was like a force.

I went to the next picture in line. And then the next, and the next, and the next, and the next.

And they told the story.

No, he wasn't the pastor nor was he preaching. In fact, Jaden Williams was dead. The picture of a closed casket being supported and marched away toward an open grave of dignity by pall bearers was a testament and confirmation of that.

But there was something else that was shocking to me that I didn't know... not until now.

Jaden Williams and my high school crush Karla Dancer had gotten married. And " SHE" was the Pastor Williams! And "SHE" was the one that I was hired to kill! Damn!

I wanted to sit. I needed to think. I forced myself to try to control my breathing or to do something that would make the room stop spinning. I couldn't. My heartbeat raced faster than what my memory and brain could keep up with. Just seeing him again did something to me. Seeing her with him made it worse.

But again, something wasn't right. I began fighting again trying to force myself not to re-live the past.

Now was the time to think of this picture line up.

All those frames, they told a story...because that's what pictures do.

They take you to places where you physically can't go... be-cause that's what pictures do.

And that's what I needed right now. I needed these pictures to do what they do.

I needed them to reach out to me. To say something to me. To speak a word to me. To grab me for Christ's sake *because that's what pictures do!!*

But I was confused. There were way too many loose pieces in these pictures. Things weren't fitting and people weren't fitting.

Wait a minute...let me get this right

Photo 1... the police officer.
Photo 2... his graduating class form the academy.
Photo 3... their wedding picture.
Photo 4... a dinner party with friends; maybe family.
Photo 5... the coffin and the pall bearers.
Photo 6... *Karla* in her wedding gown standing with her parents.

I studied... my eyes darting from picture to picture.
Searching.
Digging.
Examining.
Shoveling and shuffling.
Moving pictures around from one spot to another and back again.
Something was out of place. *Someone* was out of place.
I just couldn't figure it out. But then it suddenly hit me and I realized what it was. There *was* a clue.

That something that was out of place was a dinner party photo. Unlike all the other shots, except for one, Karla and her parent's photos didn't have any cops in it; or so it seemed.

After looking deeper something shocked me. A person shocked me. It was a person that I recognized.

Stacey Pratt. My first hit.

"What the hell was he doing in *this* picture? ...in *this* house?" I asked myself.

What was the connection?

And then the last picture.

Someone had put these pictures in this order for a reason and it looked like...

"A police line up," I whispered to myself.

Karla Dancer and her parents were the last pieces to that puzzle.

But her parents were dead now. They were killed by someone or some people other than me and those same people were still on their job and would stop at nothing until she was dead too.

I had to save her... no matter what. This was a weird twist of fate and even a weirder change of mind but I had to save the last Dancer

Chapter Six

I rushed through traffic racing to get back to the church.

I had wasted a lot of time at Karla's house and I feared that now she could be suffering, or even worse, dying because of it. There was even a strong possibilty that whoever had killed her parents could've already gotten to her. And this scared me.

I didn't have a phone number, I couldn't call her.

All I had was this road rage that was now working its way into overdrive.

"Damn!" I cursed... another stupid *bleep bleep* was in *my* way *in* the fast lane.

"Move the *Bleep* out the way!" I screamed weirdly feeling guilty about my choice of words.

It was funny to me. Not funny as in humorous but funny to me as in strange. Here I am, now, feeling guilty about a little swearing and curse words when it had been only hours earlier that I had accepted payment to murder a preacher!

"I'm sick," I told myself.

Saving the Last Dancer

Chapter Seven

All but for a few cars and a lineup of buses, the Church's parking lot was almost empty. Nothing was out of place and nothing seemed suspicious. The Pastor's car was where I had last seen it and as far as I could see there weren't any strange characters lurking around. No one was outside.

I wanted to call Michael but I couldn't because not only was I going against the grain now but I also felt awkward suddenly realizing that I didn't have his number either. He had always called me from a blocked number and up until now it never really mattered to me. That was how it worked.

I wanted to curse again but dared not...especially not on holy ground.

I sat waiting with my eyes glued to the Mercedes. As I did I further searched my mind.

The photos...

"All cops... *in a line*," I slowly said to myself.

Someone was trying to spell out *a cop line up* and all of the photos were... *framed !*

Damn... if I could just figure it out. I felt the tip of an iceberg almost about to breakthrough and manifest when...

BINGO!

MOVEMENT!

Pastor Williams came walking out the door.

I didn't want to startle nor frighten her and neither did I know if she had any idea that her life was in danger so I did everything slow.

I started my car and put it in drive.

I thought that I would've atleast known how to approach her once I got here, but how was I to tell her that her parents were dead or even convince her that I wasn't the one who kill them?

I'm halfway across the parking lot when out of nowhere and from between the parked church buses that were off to the side a blue van popped out and started hightailing it across the lot toward the Pastor as she walked toward her car.

Karla wasn't even looking.

I jammed my accelerator and blew the horn.

She turned... looked... registered all the action in her

mind... and then *froze.*

The van's side door slid open but before anything else could happen...

BAM!

My Cadillac crashed into it causing an assault rifle-toting hooligan to come flying out of it airborne and slamming onto the top of my hood as he slid across it before hitting the ground.

I jumped out, pumped two .45 caliber slugs into the goon's brain and then swung around for the driver.

He, too, was shocked.

He hadn't seen me either until the crash. But now being dazed from it, things were happening way too fast for him.

He was slowly lifting himself up and had just unglued his forehead from the van's now blood-stained steering wheel when

206

just like it happened to his *compadre*, his gook exploded too.

"Get in your car!" I shouted to Karla now running toward her.

"What's going on?" she demanded though she was still heading toward her car in hurried steps.

I was so glad that she wasn't trying to play the *shero* type right now.

"Shoot...I knew this was coming," she stated.

"Get in the passenger seat.! I'll drive!" I told her.

There was a slight hesitation at first but not much before she handed me her car keys and quickly moved around to the other side before hopping in.

I thought about what she had said 'that she *knew* that this was coming'.

"How? ...and how much did she know?" I wondered.

But Karla seemed a lot more calm than what I'd thought she'd be. And prettier. Beautiful even...in a mature way.

But she hadn't recognized me. In fact, she hadn't even looked at me yet. Even now as we drove, her eyes stayed glued to the street.

Again, I was surprised at her sereneness. She was like *way* too undisturbed for a woman who was now running for her life.

I mean, it wasn't like a *'Take me Lord, I'm ready to die'* calmness, but it wasn't an 'Oh my God please don't let me die!' type of way either. She was too hard to read.

"Do you know what this is about?" I asked now wondering why this woman wasn't calling the police.

I mean, I know damn well why *I* wasn't going to call them-- but why wasn't she? She was the one who was the law abiding upstanding citizen *and* pastor.

I drove a little further to make sure that we weren't being followed and then I pulled over.

"Now, tell me what the hell is going on," I demanded.

"No-- you first," she said in a counteracting way. "And who are you?"

Under normal circumstances I would've been crushed that she didn't recognize me... but after 15 years of military, war, sizeable weight gain, and facial hair... I wasn't tripping on.

"I was hired to kill you," I screwed up and said.

"Wrong answer," she said. And then *sppphhhhh...* This heifer sprayed me with mace! Then she grabbed for her keys and the door handle.

One hand was swiping, rubbing and trying to protect my eyes from a second possible stream, and the other was grabbing at her arm.

The passenger door was open and half of her body was already hanging out as she struggled to free herself.

"Hold on! Hold on, Karla!" I screamed. "You're safe now! I'm not trying to kill you. I'm trying to save your life!"

"Let go of me!" she screamed, "LET--GO!"

And with that this woman flung that little small ass aerosol can *sooo* hard and hit me in my lips.

DAMN!

I couldn't do nothing but let go then. My hand went straight to my mouth.

I could barely see and I *knew* that I couldn't talk at the moment but by the time that I had managed to get the driver's side door open and prepared myself for a chase I was shocked. Karla had already pushed the remote's release button for the trunk to open and had already reached in...

She came out with a .40 caliber GLOCK.

Whoa... I had forgotten that this chick's husband had been a police.

"You'd better choose your next words wisely, Mister. Because right about now I'm surely thinking about being the one who's going to preach at your funeral."

With one eye still closed *and* burning and the other spitting out tears the size of raindrops, I began speaking... slowly.

"Karla... Karla Dancer. It's me... Federick Upchurch. I came through high school with you. Remember? Scrawny little kid, in the band, tuba player, *bomp-bomp-bomp*?"

Her eyebrows went up, then she squinted...and then the barrel came level to my face.

"Yeah, I remember now... you used to stalk me."

"No, no, no, no," I said throwing my hands up, "I had a *crush* on you. I ain't *never* been no stalker."

"Then how'd you find me? Are you one of them too?"

"One of who?" I asked.

I was still searching for answers but I needed to get this gun out of her hands first, and soon.

She said nothing but she stared hard.

"Do you understand?" I asked getting ready to make my move. "Karla, I'm trying to save your life. I've already killed two guys back there at the church trying to keep you alive. Now--somebody wants you dead and I'm asking do you know why?"

The words hung in the air.

"Please, Karla. We don't have much time."

The woman of God exhaled and then lowered her aim. It was a long, hard, well overdue exhalation. I walked up to her and held my hand out for the gun. After looking me in my eyes for a second she finally handed it to me.

"I need to go home," she said. It wasn't a question. It was her car and she was already walking around to the driver's side of it.

Not wanting to get left behind I took out toward the passenger side. But what could I say right now? How was I going to tell her?

I had 15 minutes to figure it out.

The first thing was to keep her off the phone. I couldn't let her call her house. "Your phone may be bugged," I told her, "you can't use it... okay?"
Thank God she understood.

Saving the Last Dancer

Chapter Eight

A few more minutes to go before we would be arriving at her house but a few minutes wouldn't be long enough.

"I know that you married Jaden Williams," I told her, "and I know that he was a police officer."

"Okay--*soooo*, the whole city knew that."

"And that *somebody* was involved in something," I added, "and somehow you're mixed up in it all."

"I'm not mixed up in anything," she snapped, "Me and my family are innocent... and my husband had *nothing* to do with it."

Wait a minute... she said *'it'*.

'It' as in she knows what *'it'* is. But I haven't enough time to get it out of her, not while trying to prepare her for what she was about to encounter at her home.

It was now or never.

"Karla... I've been to your house."

A quick glance my way and then her eyes went back on the road.

"And my parents?" she asked me.

I said nothing.

"Mr. Upchurch... I just asked about my mother and my father. Now, I'm about two minutes away from my home. If you need to tell me something, and *if* something is wrong there-- I strongly suggest that you say something now."

"I'm sorry, Karla. The men at the church... they went *there* first."

Just as I had done earlier I suggested to Karla that she should also make a pass through the front way and come up another street. She did and after we parked we walked through the alley to the rear of her house.

Once we were inside in the kitchen I held her by the shoulders and looked her square in the eyes...

"They're with God now... He has a better place for them," I mistakenly said to her...and then *her* wrath came down.

"Don't you dare stand here and even attempt to dignify your actions with me, you hypocrite. Lest you forget, you're just as much a murderer as those others? So, you're going to hell just like the rest of them, man."

Damn, that hurt-- real bad coming from her.

But I soaked it up and took her by the hand. I led her through her own house and down the same path that I had taken earlier. I still heard Steve Harvey.

"So they were watching their recorded *Family Feud* episodes?" she asked rhetorically.

I said nothing but her statement answered my question.

Then I stopped short only a foot or so away from the doorway of her den. She knew what I was thinking and was about to say.

"Mr. Upchurch," she said stopping me before I spoke, " you can't imagine how I feel right now and neither can you *assume* how I'm going to react once I enter that door... but allow me to reassure you that unlike what you think, I've seen a lot. I've seen people die a thousand deaths in as little as the time that it took for them to get from their seats out in the congregation up until the time that it took for them to get to the altar. But I never broke. Not even when I preached my *own* husband's funeral."

And she didn't break.
I gave her space and I gave her *her*
respect. No longer was she that little high
school gallivanting teenage girl trying to
dance her way into the future.
She had arrived... with dignity... with
courage... and with strength.
I watched her as she kissed her
mother...and then her father.
She said a prayer and then it was over.

Later on I had asked her why hadn't she
cried or looked up to the heavens toward
God when she had prayed.
She told me...
"Rejoice for the ones who are gone. But
not only that, I'm done with the troubles
of the world, Upchurch. I'm the only
Dancer left now and I don't have nobody
else but God, so why look up in the sky for
Him knowing that He's right here by my
side-- like He has always been."
What could I have said after that?

It was time to go...

We had to leave and she knew it. It
wouldn't be long before cops and killers

arrived, both, suited and booted and kicking her door down.

She left the room and went somewhere in the house before returning back into the den with two large travel bags.

"What are you doing now?" she asked walking up to stand beside me.

I was back in front of those pictures.

"I don't know... trying to put a pattern to all this mess," I answered still staring at the photos.

"What kind of pattern? And why did you change my pictures around?" she asked grabbing up their wedding picture and the one of her and her parents.

"I'm confused," I said watching her as she crossed over the den to a large fireplace with an equally grandiose mantel.

There were pictures on it as well.

"First of all," she started and now walking back to the piano with a picture, "all *these* pictures are cops. And those over there on the mantel are family and wedding pictures only."

"So who moved them?" I asked now looking at the line up in a whole different light, "and don't this one belong over there with the family?"

I was pointing at the dinner party picture... Photo No. 4.

"That's not family... those are cops."

"Cops!" I damn near shouted, "All of them?"

"Yeah... every last one of 'em but me."

"What about him?" I asked and pointed... almost afraid of the answer.

"Who?...Stacey? He was a partner and a good friend of my husband's. But after Jayden had gotten a promotion to Narcotics he transferred over to Property and Evidence. Why? And why did you ask about him...you know him?"

I couldn't answer her at the time... I was still floored about Pratt being a cop.

Narcotics?

Property and Evidence?

I killed a Cop?

My gut feeling was beginning to act up again and what I was thinking I don't think I wanted to know. But still I turned and started stepping toward the last picture over on the end. The one that had replaced Photo NO. 6. The one that I hadn't seen earlier because it was on the wrong side of the room. that were all cops.

I stood there almost in shock.

I couldn't believe it. There he was as big as the morning star... *Michael!*

"You're looking like you just stared Satan in the eyes, Upchurch."

"I think I did," I told her.

Michael had been playing me all along. He set me up. He had me killing cops and everything. I was lost. The room began spinning again and my legs started melting all over. I couldn't breathe.

"Are you okay?" Karla asked.

But I couldn't answer. I ran straight for the front door. Out-side I puked all over her mother's gardenias.

I was sorry for it, ofcourse, *considering*... but hey, no disrespect intended.

Finally done, but still buckled over with my hands on my knees, I looked up just in time to see two black Suburbans heading my way... *with their lights out.*

I ran inside.

"Let's go!" I said grabbing up the two bags, "we've got to get out of here!"

We exited the way we came--through the kitchen and out the back.

Just as we were hitting the alley I heard a crash in the house and with a quick glance over my shoulder I saw beams of white lights darting to and fro crisscrossing everywhere through an upstairs bedroom window.

This was the hit squad...coming for the Pastor.

Karla was a wanted woman now.

Probably just as much as I was a wanted man.

Chapter Nine

"Cops were involved," I realize now and saying it to myself, and somehow Karla had known that.

And that's why she hadn't called the cops... *then.*

But here she was on her phone now.

I asked her, "What are you doing?"

"I'm dialing 911," she said.

"Those are cops that are back there at your house," I reminded her.

"No...those are *dirty* cops that are at my house," she corrected, "and once the call is dispatched over the radio and they hear it they'll leave before any other *real* cops get a chance to respond."

That was smart of her. Good thinking.

"And so that will also take care of your mother and your father being found and..."

"Yes it will. Until I have to go..." she thought about it first and then asked, "I'll end up having to go identify the bodies, won't I?"

"Yeah... but let's get you cleared on some of this mess first, okay?"

I drove at a speed much slower than the rate that my brain was farting out thoughts. We had to ditch this car and fast.

We had to find somewhere safe to lay low and we had to get to a television.

My car, the shootings at the church, bodies at her house...

"In an hour or so our faces are going to be plastered *all* over the news. And I'm sure that warrants are going to be put out for our arrests too," I told her.

"I know, I've been thinking about that," she replied, "any ideas?"

"Not yet," I answered.

And then my phone rang.

I had forgotten that I even had it on me.

It continued ringing as I dug it out of my pocket.

I looked at it... Blocked Caller.

"Hello," I answered knowing that it was Michael.

"You stupid dumb bastard!" he was yelling, "You're dead! You hear me? You're dead !"

I had to go in on him.

"You set me up, you son of a bitch!" I yelled back.

"You set yourself up, Beckmon -- or should I say *Upchurch*?"

My real name?

He just used my real name?

It shocked me at first but then I remembered... he was a cop.

But he said it with more than just an aire of a cop. It sounded too familiar to his voice, as if he'd been saying it for years.

He continued on.

"Upchurch, you sorry piece of shit... you bring her to me *now* before you and her both have contracts out on you."

"I'll put a price tag over your head that'll be cheaper than a fucking *40oz* of beer if you try to screw my over on this!"

"And that's supposed to insult me, motherfucker? I shot a cop!"

"No, you killed a snitch!"

I had gotten so worked up over the phone call that I had forgotten all about the preacher that was in the car with me.

"Who is that?" she asked in a whisper.

Karla listened but had no idea of who I was talking and arguing with. But she asked again as I held a hand up sig-naling for patience and trying to hear.

Thankfully she had missed the part about me shooting a cop.

"Upchurch... who *is* that?" she asked again stubbornly ignoring my plea for silence.

Michael was saying something else...

"This is way over your head, son. Take the money, hand her over, and get out. She already done talked enough. Now let's go ahead and get this thing done with before it's too late to even turn the situation around for you."

"That's a negative, *Mike*-- or whoever you are. So either come up with something better than that or sing that song to the devil... 'cause I'm coming to get you."

"And you won't have to look far... you sorry piece of shit. Believe me, I'm not hard to find."

Again, my phone line went dead. I had barely hit the "END" button before Karla tore into me with the questioning.

I interrupted her.

"Hey, who was that guy in that last picture shaking your husband's hand?'

Karla Williams closed her eyes, possibly to imagine the photo and to think about it.

"The white guy in the brown suit?" she asked.

"Yeah... that one."

"That was my husband's old boss," she answered.

"*Old* boss?" I questioned now thinking about the sequence of the pictures.

Suddenly the "Mrs." went quiet on me.

"Karla...," I began slightly upset now, "what did you mean old boss?"

"I can't tell you," she replied.

"What the...," I paused, "what do you mean 'can't tell me'?"

"I *can't* tell you," she repeated.

I was about to explode.

"You can't tell me why my life is in danger! Or why every cop in this city is on a system wide 'shoot to kill' murder for hire manhunt for me!"

Karla still didn't answer but I refused to give up on trying to get them from her. Either she knew something that she was hiding in order to protect the reputation of the good name of her late husband, or-- she was hiding something because she was afraid. Either way, I had to find out.

She was holding the key to our next move.

"That was him that I was talking to on the phone just then," I said.

"That was who?"

"The man in the picture... your husband's old boss... the same man who hired *me* to kill *you*."

She looked at me. I could tell that something was churning inside of that head of hers. She was contemplating. And then she gave me a name.

"His name is Angel McPherson... a big wig. He's in the Department's Narcotics Division."

I thought about it.

"But that's not right-- something is still wrong. He was your husband's *old* boss. So why was your husband's old boss at the end of the photo line up?"

I begin remembering that there were *two* pictures that had been replaced, and that I had only seen one, Michaels... or Angel McPherson's. That was before I had caught out toward the front door to release my innards.

But then I started thinking...what if Karla had somehow replaced the photos out of sequence? I never saw the other picture.

"Karla...," I damn near whispered. The car's interior cabin was very quiet.

"Yes, Upchurch."

She knew it was coming so I was sure that she was bracing herself.

"That other picture, " I asked feeling my heart rate increase, "who was in it? Who was the final piece of this puzzle?"

For the first time I think I heard a tremble in her voice and had it not been for me driving I would have looked at her. But that was only an excuse because I could've looked at her anyway, but I didn't.

I wanted to respect her dignity... give her space... and allow her to cry alone.

"The other picture," I repeated," who was it, Karla? "

"Jaden's new boss," she finally said.

"*New* boss?"

"Yes... new boss. William Donaldson," she said, "*Internal Affairs.*"

Chapter Ten

Stacey Pratt had gone to Jaden Williams after Jaden had started working under William Donaldson gathering information about Angel McPherson stealing evidence... namely cocaine, heroin, and guns.

"It had been happening for years-- even before me," Stacey had said trying to protect his own ass.

No one had known how deep the corruption had sunken, nor how wide it had spreaded. Jaden had been ordered and authorized to spearhead the investigation... somewhat as a double agent of sorts. His promotion and transfer had been kept *hush-hush* by his superiors and he was left in his old division.

Same job, same title, same everything... however, added duties which were: report everything directly to Donaldson.

McPherson and his band of licensed killers had worked with and around

Williams for well over a year before they finally began trusting him.

They approached him through Pratt. He was their inside man... he was also Williams' ex-partner.

As much as Williams had wanted to tell Pratt about his assignment and his new promotion , strict orders on confidentiality had prevented him from doing so--friend or not, he had to wait.

But Jaden never got a chance to tell Stacy, and sadly, Stacy never got a chance to give his statement. Pratt was never found. He just disappeared...like *poof!* But that *poof* came from the other end of my rifle. Stacey had tried taking days off...hiding out . He knew that his career in the department had come to an end.

They found him and they sent me to do their dirty work.

Karla and I pulled into a small two-for-fifteen rinky dink cheap motel.

"Oh my God, "she said, "you come here often?"

She almost got a "*hell no*" out of me but when I looked over at her she had a cross and a prayer cloth in her lap.

I refrained.

Minutes later, returning to the car after a fierce negotiating session with the motel's manager, I pulled up in front of a door that had two tarnished looking numbers nailed to it that read 23.

I thought of Jordan.

"Honey... we're home," I sung out trying to lighten the moment.

Karla forced a weak smile and got out of the car.

Inside the room we made small talk keeping everything simple until we had both settled our nerves.

"Before we get down to some serious planning, Upchurch, I need to change," she told me.

Karla grabbed the smallest one of the two bags that she had me bring in with us and went into the bathroom. I sat in a chair wondering what the other one contained. It had been the larger and the heaviest of the two had given me immediate concern and curiosity.

Finally after what had seemed like eternity Karla returned.

Whoa !

I was doing my *damndest* at being as respectful as possible with the good ol' Pastor but as soon as she emerged through that restroom door the old me, *that ol' lustful man*...almost, if not only but for a minute, resurfaced.

Growing up I had overheard older church guys jokingly say as they gathered around in the parking lot watching the "sisters" get out of their cars to go in for service that it was only natural that a man should look at a woman.

" Yeah, but two looks are one too many," one of the oldest of the guys had said, " that first natural glance is for you... That second on-- well, that one is the devil."

Thinking about it now as I stared at this woman in these tight grey sweats pants and tank top, I must've stole a glance *or* two for not only myself, but for Satan that ol' devil... *his* homeboy and a couple of his little fire starting ass workers too.

This woman hadn't lost it at all. The woman was just as fine now as she was way back in high school... if not finer.

(But, ofcourse the comparisons now were definitely judged by grown man standards.)

She noticed my stare.

"Excuse me, *Brother* Upchurch... if you don't mind, would you please keep your eyes above shoulder level?"

"Oh, my bad...*Pastor*," I told her stealing one more look.

"Mmm-hmm... whatever."

She immediately took out walking toward that one bag that was left on the bed... the big one. The one I was curious about.

"Jaden told me that if anything were to ever happen to him. If he got killed, kidnapped, arrested, came up missing... anything-- that I should go in the attic, grab this bag, and run."

"What's in it?" I asked.

"I don't know," she said unzipping it.

I watched as the first thing that she pulled out was a box of shells, and then four more.

Next were two 9mm pistols.

A micro digital recorder.

A big roll of money...I saw large bills.

Two cell phones... probably untraceable.

And an envelope.

I could see that there were other things still in the bag, but Karla stopped digging at that time and opened the envelope.

She sat on the bed beside the bag and quietly read.

I watched intently as I attempted to make out the expressions of her face. They went from calmness to concentration back to calmness but ended with *intense* concentration.

It wasn't until she had finished and begun stuffing the letter back into its envelope that I noticed a touch of sadness in her spirit.

"Are you okay?' I asked her.

"I'll be fine," she promised. "The letter said that there were a bunch of files in the bag with dates, information, and photo shots. Evidence on everyone that's involved. Enough to put them all away."

She lifted out a stack and began reading through the names aloud. Some were recognized but most weren't.

She read out a Richards, a Newton, an Owens, Jones, McPherson's, Pratt... and then she stopped and looked up at me.

"What?" I asked curious as to the look upon her face.

Slowly she handed me a file.

"What the hell?" I said.

I was shocked. My eyes burned with disbelief as I tried to make out the letters before me. It had to be some kind of joke. No way... this couldn't be true.

I looked back up at Karla.

The file read: FEDERICK UPCHURCH.

I read the file.

I was amazed and confused all at the same time.

It contained my entire military jacket... all the way back to my date of enlistment.

Deployment dates, duty stations, assignments and duties, ribbons, awards... hell, it even had the documentation date of my release and discharge.

"I can't believe this, Karla, "I said still speechless and still reading.

I stood and paced as I did.

"I don't know what to make of it either," she told me, "I thought that you didn't know my husband? Were you mixed up in all this bullcrap too?"

"Hell no, " I said without thinking," I mean, *no*. I wasn't in this stuff and I *didn't* actually know your husband except for back in our high school days. I don't even know how he got this information. "

"You knew something," she almost yelled, "he had a file on you."

"So! And as I've said 'I don't know how he got it'!"

"And who do you call yourself yelling at?" she asked almost borderline upset as well.

"Why? Because you are all so self-righteous that I can't holler at you... or fight back when you judge me and make those crazy ass accusations as if I was a part of that same bullshit that your crooked ass husband was a part of?"

Karla stepped right up to me and slapped me. I took it.

She slapped me again and I didn't budge.

I stood in front of her now absorbing blows to the chest one after the other until they ceased allowing her to morph into a small broken-hearted little girl again. And then I held her as she cried the tears of a million souls.

Saving the Last Dancer

Chapter Eleven

She hadn't even known that Pratt was dead. There was no way that I could tell her that I was the one who had killed him. But I wasn't alone in my sin.
Life had Killed Him.
McPherson had killed him.
The department, and later on, Jaden Williams had killed him.
But my profession had killed him as well... I was a sniper... which is what had bothered me about the file that Jaden had on me.
I didn't want to tell Karla because I didn't want her being more terrified than what she was right now. And though she was doing one hell of a job at hiding it, I believe more pressure would've really done it right now--as far as breaking her.

We sat down, put all the files on the bed and began reading them. Within an hour we were convinced of who the enemies were.

We had enough information on all the players in the game, so now was the time to blow the whistle.

We spent the next hour putting our plan together. But something was still bothering me...

I was an elite, upper level security clearance, trained sniper. I even went by a different name in the military. I traveled places on assignment under an alias that should've never been discovered, released, documented or known by any *regular* cop.

In short, Jaden Williams should've never even known that my life existed, *except* for high school.

After that it should've appeared that I was dead, lost, missing, AWOL, anything other than what was documented.

I had to find out more. But how? And how was I to keep what I do and had done away from Karla?

There had to be a way.

Chapter Twelve

Getting down to business...

Though I didn't lie, I never really answered Karla when she had asked me about the motel. No, I didn't come often... but the manager and I did have history. She was Chinese and a good friend of mine that I had named Chu-Chu, her last name being Chu of course.

Chu-Chu's Motel normally rented for the popular fee of two hours for fifteen dollars, but because of all of my much needed extras, that fifteen dollars had ballooned up to fifteen *hundred* dollars... and that was even after negotiating.

But the fee included having Pastor Williams' car stored in a garage to the rear of the motel where Chu-Chu actually lived.

It also included the rental of an old dropped down, souped up, super loud, but slow, race car looking Honda Civic that her incarcerated son had been driving since high school... he was now 30.

We loaded up the little pocket rocket and headed out. Jaden's little survival kit had also included a fake ID for Karla with an accompanying pre-loaded credit card.

We were set for now but we still had to lay low for a few hours in order to give our plans some time to hatch. The wheels were set in motion.

First stop... a 24hour business center or somewhere where we could use a computer, a scanner, a fax, etc.

"How about a Hilton?" she had asked.

"I'm good with that," I told her knowing that the prepaid credit card had been a damn good idea that her departed husband had thought of.

She looked uncomfortable sitting over there in the Honda's passenger seat. Me...I was cool.

I had been in a lot more uncomfortable situations and positions than this. This was daycare compared to some of my assignments... and first class compared to some of my methods of transportation.

I asked her, "You okay?"

She was digging out the two cell phones that had been left by Jaden and their power cords.

"These things are dead, "she said... my eye twitched from the mere mention of the word *dead*.

"We'll be there soon. Go ahead and cut our other phones off, "I reminded her.

I had wanted them to stay on and transmitting as we rolled around for a while. It was a test.

If our phones were bugged or being tracked by GPS I purposely rode around everywhere while constantly checking and staying in my rearview mirror. I was checking for a tail. Had there been one eventually they would have fouled up and I would have spotted them.

Everything was clear.

I didn't mind my phone being cut off now, there was no need to keep the line open waiting on McPherson... hell, thanks to Jaden's investigation and files I had all the information that I need on that snake... and I had his phone number now, too.

Ten minutes later we were pulling into the hotel. Karla went and paid for the room...double beds of course and I brought in the bags.

I had also told her to check out the Front Desk's night clerk to see if he'd fit into the plan that she and I had devised. She came back and said, "Yes... he was perfect."

She had kind of balked at first about *that* part of the plan but eventually I had convinced her.

One quick stop at the always convenient 24hour *Walmart* had gotten us what we were going to need when the time came.

Room time...

The key card slid and the little red indicator light turned green. We entered...

"Well, "Karla began already, "not quite my standards but it's at least better than that last dump you had us in."

"You sure seem to have a lot of insight about motel grades to be a woman of the cloth," I joked and stabbed at her.

She shot a glance my way.

"Whatever, brother... I know that devil *is* a lie."

I laughed.

Another two hours and we'd be ready. I flopped down on the bed furthest from the door and began taking off my shoes. Karla went into the bathroom to brush her teeth. I had asked her while we were out if she was hungry or wanted anything to eat, but like myself, she had no appetite.

I was tired.

By the time she resurfaced from the bathroom this time I was asleep.

Saving the Last Dancer

Chapter Thirteen

It was time to get things going.

Karla had woke me up as requested and when she did, it shocked me.

I almost had to burst out laughing. This was the part of the plan that she *didn't* like.

"Yeah- -yeah, I know... it's a dirty job but somebody's got to do it," I joked.

Karla had spent the better part of the last hour getting her attire and make-up together. She was already a beautiful woman to begin with... so with all the added lashes, lipstick, liners and gloss-- she was now perfect to play the part of a hoochie... a hooker...or rather, a woman of the night.

"I look like a harlot, " she complained through a pair of shiny lips.

"Well *duuhhh*, Pastor... that was the plan wasn't it?"

"*Your* plan... I still say that we could've pulled it off without this mess."

We argued about it a little bit longer but I had eventually won. She finally saw it my way.

Okay... step two.
Front desk...
Little Dorky Jr....
Ms. Helpless...
Ten minutes...that's all I needed.
I couldn't wait to see this.

The elevator door opened and out came long hair, perfume, and heels.
Karla's prance was a work of art.
She was wearing a very short mini-skirt, that had it not been for the tights underneath that she had insisted on wearing, would've been *very* revealing. But as much as I had wanted the legs and the thighs she had made me make a choice.
"Legs... or cleavage," she had asked, "which one, cowboy?"
Well... she was a pastor. And the bible did mention something about a woman's bosom, so... I went with that.

Her heels made loud tapping noises as she stepped through the tiled area and up to the desk.

"*Hey* sweetie... haven't seen you here before," Karla said flirting with the guy, "How long you been working here? "
"*Theven* years, " he answered.
Little Dorky Jr. was a skinny little kid with glasses and a *lisp*.
"Oh really?" Ms. Helpless said with an airhead giggle, "well, don't you get tired of working here... especially at night with no one here to talk to?"
"*Thometime*. But can I help you though, Ma'am? "
Karla went into the act.
"Why of course you can, baby,"
Karla said this and then leaned over the counter. Little Dorky Jr.'s eyes went straight down to her breast and back up again.
"You see--I know that this may be asking for a little too much, but can you come up to my room for a sec, I *really* need some help up there."
I stood from a distance watching. I had slipped down the stairwell and as I waited all I could do was just sit back and enjoy

the show until it was my time to hit the stage.

Karla waited for his answer.

"I'm not *thuppo* to leave the area," he said.

Karla reached over and ran a fingernail across his name tag.

"Look... Theo," and because she actually wanted to laugh, she asked the Lord for forgiveness, "I won't tell anybody if you don't."

Minutes later they were outside of our room door fumbling with the demagnetized card key that I had also included as a prop in our plan.

But I was downstairs working as fast as I could scanning, faxing, and emailing documents and evidence all over the place.

I had to work fast... warp speed.

Little Dorky Jr. didn't know what to expect from this lady once he had gotten upstairs. Of course he had remembered that Karla had checked in alone, so... maybe he thought he'd get lucky.

"This key *theem* to be *mesth* up," he said now on his third or fourth try.

Pastor Williams was doing a good job at keeping him busy but something unexpected happened... Dorky Jr. had brought a Master key with him.

"Leth thee if *thith* one work," he said surprising her.

Karla was caught off guard by it but kept her composure.

She couldn't believe that we had actually missed something so small as the possibility of him bringing an extra key card.

"What about a backup plan?" she thought to herself, "we didn't think about this."

Quick to think on her feet she thought of her own.

"Oh my! You got it opened!" she exclaimed, "You wanna come in?"

Little Dorky quickly answered, " *thure--* I *guesth* I got a little time."

Pastor Williams wanted so bad to get the little guy behind that door and break out her anointing oil and just literally splash it all over him. By the time she'd let him out of there he'd been speaking in tongues for real.

"The nerve of him, " she steamed inside, " looking at me like I'm some kind of laylow truckstop lot lizard... JESUS, you'd better get him!"

I was in luck... just as I had hoped Little Dorky Jr. had been logged on to the hotel's computer and email account. Some-thing that I had wanted and definitely *needed*. I sent off everybody's file that I had copied, scanned or faxed to other pertinent destinations and then to someone in their circle other than themselves.

That was going to create and cause a web of phone calls, and with all the chaos someone was sure to mess up and say something incriminating.

I had sent McPherson's file to Newton, Newton's file to Richards, Richards to Owens, and so on. And I sent everybody's to McPherson... all but my own and Pratt's. I had left him out of the equation. My little gift, letting him rest in peace I guess.

Now I was on the hotel's actual phone line calling this Donaldson guy from internal affairs *and* the FBI.

It was time to bust this case wide open.

Donaldson had already knew just about everything but I was now explaining , as fast as I could, everything to a Special Agent of the Federal Bureau of Investigations; a man whose card had also been placed in the bag left by Jaden.

I ran down all the phone numbers that I had on each of the men from the files.

"In simple terms," he was telling me, "we've already been cleared and given authorization for these phone lines. It's a *go* on the emergency phone taps. "

I felt a wave of relief.

"See you soon," the Government man told me and then he added, "... and be careful soldier."

"I will, Sir."

And the line went dead.

My job was done here. Time to head back upstairs now.

By the time that I had got there and back in the room, of course I used a *good* key card, I was shocked by the miracle that had transpired during the time of my absence.

Pastor Williams had a washcloth in her hand and was still wiping away at a face that had already been stripped bare of *any* traces of makeup. There was no lipstick, lip liner, lip gloss... nothing. And I'm sure that she had all but *snatched* those fake eyelashes off the moment she stepped back in the room... those were probably the *first* to go.

On the other hand... Little Dorky Jr. whom the Pastor had ordered for me to start calling Marcus Shelby, or rather, Brother Shelby was just finishing up a prayer and getting to his feet as I was walking in.

"Praise God... *I'm thaved now!*" he was saying as he grabbed me up in a big ol' happy hug.

I felt awkward but I understood everything, especially when I noticed a big shiny spot of oil all over his forehead.

"Now remember," she was telling him as she walked him to the door, "what I told you is just between you, me, and Jesus. Okay? Now you call me as soon as those men get in the elevator. "

"Okay, *Pathor*... just me, you and *Jethuth*."

Karla smiled and told the kid, "and you can always call Him up and tell Him what you want."

Brother Shelby left.

Saving the Last Dancer

Final Chapter

Hitting the fan...

I knew that Hell was coming and had tried to prepare myself for it.

I closed my eyes and prayed... quickly.

Pastor Williams was ready too. All the pieces were in place and instincts told me that they were near... *Everyone.*

"Are you gonna be okay?" I asked Pastor.

I was about to leave to go downstairs. It was part of the plan.

She had to stay upstairs and wait on my signal from down in the lobby. She seemed scared... but she looked brave.

"Jesus got me, "she smiled and said.

And then I was gone.

After fifteen nerve wrecking minutes of trying to seem and look calm sitting in the lobby, through large plate glass windows that separated the breath that I was now breathing from the air that there was a possibility that I would never breathe again, I could see and counted four black Suburbans pulling up.

All came to a stop and all four doors on all four vehicles flew open. Men poured out of each.

My muscles tightened.

I dialed McPherson's phone number.

I watched from where I was sitting as "*Michael*" answered his phone.

"Hello, Michael, "I said.

"Mr. Beckmon," he answered signaling for his men to stand down. "Nice to be back on speaking terms and first name bases with you."

Even his lies were sarcastic.

"Some things don't last forever," I counter-amused as I watched him pointing men toward the front door. "No need for that, Michael. I'm in the Front Lobby. "

I saw and heard him whistle to his guys signaling for them to stop again.

"You're playing games, Beckmon."

"No... I'm making deals," I answered and offered.

"Okay...then, let's make a deal--I'm listening. But talk quick, my guys are getting cold out here. "

"Everyone know everyone else's business, right? No one can cross anybody out from this point. That's why all the emails. I want it to all stop here. No one else dies, McPherson."

"Okay. You got my attention. Keep going...what's next?"

I took a breath because the next part was sneaky...

"Next..." I began, "the church lady walks with me."

"Can't do that, Beckmon... you know she knows too much. Plus she's got files. "

"No! I have the files now and without em' her word means nothing! "

Silence fell upon the open line.

Maybe he was considering, maybe he was stalling.

Underneath my shirt I felt for my .45 . It felt cold to my touch.

"And what if I say no?" he tested.

"And what if I say that I'm not accepting a..."

Suddenly I could see *Michael* ending our phone call.

"GO! GO! GO! " he was shouting to his team.

I rushed to dig out my gun, but... it was too late.

Click- Clack, I heard and froze.

I had heard that sound way too many times to *not* know what it was and what it meant.

"Don't even think about it, Mr. Upchurch," I heard a somewhat familiar voice demand, " now pull the gun out slow, place it on the floor, stand and turn around."

I did as I was told...slowly.

I laid my gun on the floor... stood... and with my hands up I turned to face my fear.

Karla Williams stood with a gun aimed and placed to her head.

She was crying.

"William Donaldson? You...? Internal Affairs?" I asked.

I had *thought* that I had recognized his face from the pictures at Karla's house. His was on top of the piano too.

Jaden's *new* boss and now I was putting the face with the voice.

Not from any recent conversations, but from a con-versation months and months and months ago. He had been the man who had initially gotten me interested and into the whole *"hitman"* thing to begin with. But I had forgotten him... until now.

"You offered me a job... a long time ago. So you *knew* that I was discharging and coming back here? "

"Had you tagged a long time ago. Even ran the idea by the *Boy Wonder* Jaden. I was gonna make you guys partners. Special Assignments only. You two together would've been hometown heroes. But as you know...he was on to something else. "

"So, how did you find me again?" I asked.

"Son, you've been followed since the day you stepped foot back in this city."

"And my phone? McPherson calling me? "

"That's my line of business, Federick."

And that was how those phone calls had first begun. I chose my next questions carefully.

"And what about the photos on the piano at the house? When did you switch them out?"

After the funeral, I rode back in the family car with Williams' wife back to their house where I waited for the right opportunity and just switched them out. You can say that I *took myself out the picture,*" he said laughing.

"Thus leaving McPherson to take the fall, huh?"

Donaldson didn't take the bait.

He knew that I was probably trying to play him and McPherson against one another knowing that McPherson and his boys were standing right behind him. And he was right, they *were* behind him... but in Federal custody.

Each of his men had FBI Agents' guns accurately aimed at their heads, point blank.

The Government men had made it here and staked out the place long before Donaldson and McPherson had.

And Karla had been ready.

The new Christian convert Brother Marcus Shelby had kept his word with the Pastor and called her as soon as those *Government* men had gotten in the elevator. Just like he, she and Jesus had discussed.

"Send one of your men up to go get those copied files, McPherson," Donaldson ordered but there was no answer.

"McPherson," he said turning around...and then, "...*FUCK!*"

Everything happened so fast.

Donaldson's eyes widened with shock and fright.

Infrared beams registered dominance over his body.

Karla's elbow dug a sharp, bone crackling blow into a side of his ribs. At almost the same moment she fell to the ground and pulled one of those 9mm pistols from her waistband.

Stupidly he took an aim.

Defensively she took a shot.

And the battle between good and evil was won.

I pulled the digital recorder free from my pocket and handed it to Special Agent In Charge Hanson. Donaldson's confession was on it.

"You two have done a fine job," he told us and then apologized to Karla for her husband's death which actually and truly sounded to be sincere condolences.

She thanked him.

It wasn't until later on when Karla had confided in me and expressed to me her sadness toward the fact that Donaldson had neither confessed to nor indicated anyone else in the murder of her husband.

I felt her pain, but I felt it for a different reason.

"I'm afraid that I'll never know," she told me.

But *I* knew... and had known for a while, but I didn't want to tell her.

Didn't want to be the one to hurt her heart again. I refused to. Demons were meant to be buried—and most, buried by their own.

I fought to remain quiet about it but could no longer harbor my deception in fullness.

I called out softly to my high school crush...

"Karla... I know who killed your husband."

She wondered if she had heard me right as she stared into my soul with want.

"Who?" she calmly asked.

I walked over to the piano and lifted the picture of the dinner party.

"He's dead now," I told her, "I killed him."

"Stacey?" she asked bewildered with tears already forming in her eyes.

I lied and nodded my head.

Karla cried herself to sleep that night. Myself?

Well...I just laid there and held her in my arms all night.

I was thankful and proud to finally be able to call her *mine*.

It took fifteen long years to get her, but I did.

I thought back.

Donaldson had been the man to contact me. He had also been the man that I had talked to and that had paid me to do a job for him months and months ago... but I didn't know that the guy that he had ordered me to kill was a cop... *Jaden Williams.*

Jaden had been the problem that he had foreseen. So... I took the pay, I took the job and I took the life... her husband's life. But by some weird act of luck or miraculous intervention Donaldson never even mouthed a word about it tonight. Maybe it was because no one actually knew, or wanted to know, as long as it wasn't *them* that had actually pulled the trigger.

But they had killed him, too...we all had killed him. Only she can never find out that *I* had killed him for them.

I closed my eyes and tried to pray again but nothing came.

At that time my phone rang.

Easing out of the bed I walked over to the bathroom and closed the door behind me.

It was a blocked call.

"Beckmon," I answered.

It was another job... and I accepted it.

I wondered as I got back in bed and snuggled back up to my unsuspecting sleeping beauty of how I would forever man-age to keep this up without her ever knowing about it... *and* never learning the truth.

The truth?

That I would forever be what I am right now... A HITMAN.

And remember, there *are* no dumb snipers.

The End

Thank you for your support

For comments or to contact the
author, email us at:

and-so-l-write@hotmail·com
or
alibipubandent@gmail·com

Facebook

A.e. Santi
or
ALIBI PUBLISHING AND ENTRTAINMENT

Printing, publishing and distributing
made possible through

Alibi Publishing and Entertainment

A.e. Santi is brilliant at storytelling. His short stories are riveting and delightfully exciting. Though sometimes borderline and edgy he accents his style of writing by not being afraid to touch on certain subjects or by being down to earth enough to reach all audiences. Each page often provokes thought, laughter, anger, and mostly understanding. You won't get lost in his words or plots. Far from simple he labels his art as Entertainment Literature. Each human emotion will often be experienced and touched by the end of any one of his many superbly written page-turners. But don't sleep on him nor his future nor any of his full-scale novels...some of his best work is yet to come.

Born and raised in Oak Cliff, an inner city suburb of Dallas, Texas, he grew up as a middle child but in a very challenging household. A household different enough that looking back today gives him the ability to dig deep within to pour out his feelings, fears, faith, fashion senses and the facts. He paints his life onto the pages that he writes and shares with his readers.

He's also a God fearing man... smart enough to know where his gift comes from, strong enough to use it to its fullest potential, and humble enough to give thanks for it.

To the world of readers out there: Welcome your new friend into your home, your library, and your heart. Sit down a minute. Rest yourselves between the sheets and pages of a movie written out. You'll be glad that you did. Thanks. You all are the ones who make things happen.

Remember always... Be Blessed and Be Awesome

Made in the USA
Columbia, SC
12 July 2017